POW

Two people who were used to always being in control, Anna and Neil had to find a power balance between them—and then there was Chris to consider...

POWER POINT

BY

ROWAN KIRBY

MILLS & BOON LIMITED
15–16 BROOK'S MEWS
LONDON W1A 1DR

First published in Great Britain 1986
by Mills & Boon Limited

© Rowan Kirby 1986

Australian copyright 1986
Philippine copyright 1986
This edition 1986

ISBN 0 263 75304 2

Set in Monophoto Times 10 on 10 pt.
01–0386 – 61155

Made and printed in Great Britain by
Richard Clay (The Chaucer Press) Ltd,
Bungay, Suffolk

For Ruth and Stuart
(a vital connection)

CHAPTER ONE

RUSH hour traffic crawled and fumed, nose to tail along a major road through north London. Most of the drivers stared gloomily ahead, ignoring the early sunlight which streamed down on to metal and glass. But the young woman behind the wheel of a brown Chevette smiled to herself, bright hazel eyes shining to see this tangible proof of spring.

Reaching a relatively peaceful side street, the car detached itself from the throbbing mass to turn left, then drove on past the usual Victorian terraces in various states of gentrification and delapidation. It finally halted outside an ugly, square, prefabricated building which had been botched into a gap between two of the old houses, perhaps torn there by war damage. The place looked like what it was: an institution, set up years ago as a temporary measure and expected to move before long to more dignified permanent premises, but finding itself still there and likely to stay that way for years to come as a result of cuts in Health and Social Services. It was staffed by dedicated people who were far too busy to pause for complaint about their makeshift working environment.

As soon as the car was neatly parked in the small forecourt, the driver's door burst open and the young woman jumped out to stand on the tarmac. She reached over to the passenger seat for her bag and a bulky document case in worn leather, slammed and locked her door and set off briskly towards the entrance. She cut a striking figure with her shapely generous frame carried upright and purposeful, long legs striding out in olive green corduroy trousers tucked into high brown boots, briefcase grasped firmly under one arm, bag slung carelessly over the opposite shoulder to swing free against her black woollen jacket as she marched across the yard. Rays of sunshine caught at her hair, picking out deep blue tones in its rich lustrous raven. In colour and texture it was eye-catching, but it had been cropped into a simple style, taming her crowning glory to a cap of softly shaped layers, waving to frame her rather long face.

Her skin was surprisingly pale by contrast, totally free of make-up but glowing with a natural vitality of its own. Her features were fine and regular: the nose straight, the chin prominent and full of character, the wide mouth slightly wistful, the cheekbones high and clearly defined. Beneath the delicate dark brows, drawn together now into a faint frown, those clear gold-brown eyes held a look of deep thought, intense preoccupation, as if the mind inside was exceptionally active and probably overloaded.

Her name was Anna, she was twenty-nine years old and she worked at this somewhat tatty establishment. In fact it was the core, the pivot of her whole life.

She was one of those rare beings who combine a brilliant intelligence with a very real innocence. There was no artfulness about her. She was only dimly, uncomfortably aware of her own physical impact, which was considerable. She dressed with an instinctive style, a natural grace, to please herself rather than the dictates of fashion. Over the years, without really thinking about it, she had perfected an outer image which presented the world with a study in cool efficiency. But stirring the surface, pushing irrepressibly up from underneath, came tantalising hints of a softness, a radiant warmth. If you looked closely, it was obvious she kept them both under tight control, but not without a struggle which sometimes grew into a fierce battle inside her.

Reaching the short flight of steps leading to the glass-panelled front door, she paused briefly to study a familiar notice on the wall. It was a habit of hers, as if to remind herself where she fitted in to the place. INNER LONDON EDUCATION AUTHORITY, it announced firmly; then it went on to explain that this clinic was one of the area's Child Guidance Units, run by the School Psychological Service. Even the sign, like the rest of the outfit, was getting old, scruffy and faded, but Anna found it strangely reassuring, like a reliable old friend.

She ran up the steps and pushed the door open. A narrow hallway gave on to a reasonably spacious waiting room, currently empty, lined with long benches topped with blue plastic cushions and strewn with outdated magazines and comics. An effort had been made to soften the institutional effect with pictures and posters and some healthy potted plants which were tended lovingly and proficiently by Pam, the secretary, whose organising genius saw that the whole place ran smoothly.

Anna's eyes went straight to the clock on the wall, which told her it was 9.35. Hearing the click of the front door, Pam emerged from her inner office. She had long ago decided that it was important to greet every new arrival with a calm smile, and as a soothing start to therapy sessions this couldn't be beaten. Now her friendly middle-aged features relaxed into a broad grin as she sat down in her corner behind the reception desk, reaching for a hefty appointments diary.

'Morning, Anna. You look a bit rushed! There's no need—you're not late.' She glanced up at the clock. 'Well, only five minutes, and the first clients aren't booked till ten.'

'Hallo, Pam. I suppose I'm last in as usual?' Anna leaned on the counter-top, trying to read the open page of the diary upside down. It was dated Monday, April 18th, and divided into three columns, headed *Dr Daniel Davidson*, *Dr Anna Coleman* and *Mrs Gillian Plaistow*. Anna focused her attention on the middle column. It looked dauntingly full, even at this angle; she felt exhausted just contemplating it. 'What delights have you got lined up for me today—let's see?'

Pam's reply was cryptic. 'Hope you've had a refreshing weekend?'

'Quiet, as usual. Why?' Anna's dark brows lifted. 'Is

it that bad?' She swivelled the big book round so that she could get a proper look, pushing back the glossy fringe off her forehead with one slim hand. 'God yes, of course, Mondays, never a dull moment ... let me see ...' She ran her index finger down the list, frowning in concentration. 'Browne, Jarrett, Giles ... I was expecting those. Little Tim Browne must be about ready to make the big break, surely. He's been coming on really well ...'

She was muttering, thinking aloud. Pam did not interrupt, being quite used to such abstract tendencies in her professional colleagues; but under cover of sorting out some papers nearby, she was watching Anna closely. Anna was deeply absorbed in preparing herself for the morning's sessions ahead, but if she had glanced up just then, she might have caught an expression of caution, even concern, on the older woman's face.

'So, Janet Foster's back, is she?' Anna's finger had crossed the line that signified the break between morning and afternoon sessions. 'Hmmm, thought we'd seen the last of that one ... *hey*!' She interrupted her own murmurings with an explosion so sudden that it startled even the placid Pam, who had been half expecting it. 'What the hell does *this* mean?'

Pam's eyes followed Anna's pointing finger, though she knew perfectly well what it was pointing at. 'I was about to tell you. Your all-time favourite seems to be with us again. Oh, and Daniel wants to see you about it; now, or at lunchtime.' Her mouth twisted into a wry smile. 'Sorry, I should have warned you first.'

Anna was still staring at the last name in her list for the day. 'Tyrell! But ... does that mean *Christopher* Tyrell? I thought he ...'

'I'm afraid it does. I know you thought you'd got rid of him once, but he appears to have turned up again. It was a last-minute inclusion; they 'phoned from the social services on Friday afternoon—you left early, remember? They said it was very urgent. I couldn't refuse. I asked Daniel, and he said ...'

'But surely he doesn't have to go back on to *my* list, does he?' In her agitation, Anna drummed her fingers on the counter-top, her normally low voice rising by several tones. 'Couldn't Daniel or Gill take him on this time? Why me?'

Pam shrugged, but her eyes were sympathetic. 'You know Daniel always says it's bad form to hand over a case to someone else without good reason.'

Anna's already pale cheeks were creamy white, her eyes filmed with anxiety, her mouth trembling a little. It took a lot to shake her customary composure, but apparently this piece of news had succeeded. 'But it's hardly an existing case! I mean, it must have been— what? A year ago? And I only saw him about four or five times altogether.' With an acute effort, she regained her equilibrium. 'What's the trouble now, do you know?'

'Well, they didn't tell me the details, of course. But it'll all be in the file. If you take it now, you'll have time to study it. He's obviously still truanting, and I think I heard the social worker say something to Daniel about the lad getting into bad company ... I'm not sure, Anna, but I think ...' she leaned closer, her voice dropping to a conspiratorial whisper, 'there might have been something about drugs.'

'Drugs? Oh no!' Anna sighed wearily. 'Not that! Poor kid!' Then her features hardened into unexpected anger. 'I *knew* it was a mistake to drop those sessions. I *told* that pig-headed man—stupid, arrogant fool, throwing his weight about, dragging Christopher away just as I was making a little headway!' As if overwhelmed by an invisible outside force, her cheeks suddenly burned, her eyes blazed, her fists clenched. 'I've never in my life, before nor since, met anyone so—so bloody stubborn!'

Pam veiled a slight smile. 'Language, Dr C! We all know how you felt at the time, but perhaps the big brother won't be around this time to interfere ...'

'Huh!' Anna was far from hopeful about that. 'He'll be putting his oar in, you can bet on it. Telling us how to do our job. Never mind the fact that the poor boy got like that in the first place partly *because* big brother wasn't around as much as he might have been. Men like him make me sick! They think they can have it all their way . . .'

Pam was bustling about now, filling in a form. 'Can't be easy for him, Anna, bringing up the boy on his own. I mean, it's not like being a parent, is it? Being a parent's tricky enough; I should know!' She grinned. 'I expect whatsisname—the older brother, I've forgotten what he called himself—anyway, I expect he's doing his best.'

'Neil,' Anna supplied at once, her face expressionless.

'Neil, that was it.' Pam nodded sagely. 'A nice-looking man, as I recall. Pity he was so difficult.'

'*Difficult?* He was absolutely impossible! He made my blood boil! The one ray of sunshine about the whole mess was that I thought I'd seen the last of him. Letting Christopher go was a wrench, but at least it meant . . .' She sighed and hunched her shoulders. 'Oh well; I'd better go and see Daniel quick before the first customers arrive. Thanks for—you know—telling me, Pam.'

'Don't forget your files.' Pam indicated three trays, each bearing one of the three names that had been in the diary, and each piled up with folders. 'And if you're going to see Daniel now, could you take his through, please? They weren't ready when he arrived. I won't send anyone through to either of you till you buzz me that you're ready, okay?'

'Okay.' Anna picked up both lots of files and shoved them into her already bulging briefcase. 'See you later, then.'

'Don't worry,' Pam advised as Anna turned away, pushing the swing door which led through to the corridor of individual consulting rooms. 'You'll cope.'

'I should know all about keeping an emotional distance from my clients, after all this time,' Anna remarked, halfway through the door. 'Three years I've been here, and I still sometimes lose all that precious detachment Daniel goes on about.'

'But not often.' Pam, who had been there at least four times as long, sent her a reassuring smile. Then she stood up to welcome the first client of the day, who was hesitantly peering round the corner from the hall, accompanied by her equally nervous mother. Anna escaped hastily down the corridor.

It was hard work, but rewarding, being part of a small, supportive, competent team. Sometimes Anna thought it would be marvellous to work in a larger establishment, with a full range of talents and facilities at her disposal. But then again, there was something very satisfying about being here at the grass roots, working with the young people right in the middle of their own environment. And she did get on well with her colleagues at the Unit. There was plump, motherly Gill Plaistow—warm, wise, intuitively understanding— an experienced counsellor but not a trained psychologist like herself. Gill worked mornings only, fitting in the part-time hours with the demands of a lively family. Then there was Daniel Davidson, the boss, the psychiatrist of the outfit: large and lumbering, gentle and kindly, with his thatch of grey hair and his heavy- framed spectacles. Anna had very soon discovered that underneath that comforting exterior lurked a mind that was amazingly—sometimes alarmingly—sharp and perceptive.

She knocked on his door now, waited for his gruff 'Come!' and went in. He looked up from his desk, smiling, bushy grey brows beetling together over his glasses. 'How goes it, Anna? Good weekend? Do anything nice?'

Anna dumped her briefcase on his desk, took out his files and handed them to him. Then she sat down in his client's chair opposite him. 'Nothing special. Just quiet, you know. I had a few cases to look over, notes to write, and that report for the people at the Tavistock about . . .'

'Don't you ever stop?' He was very fond of Anna, and worried about her. It was all very well being dedicated to one's work, but she had so little else to

balance it with. As far as he could make out, her private
life was a vacuum. She existed for her career. He had
every sympathy with women's determination to keep
their place in the professional world: his wife was a
teacher, and they had always shared all the domestic
responsibilities. But they could take it too far—and in
his opinion, by cutting out any personal life, they only
succeeded in detracting from themselves as human
beings. Anna was an excellent Child Psychologist and
did her job expertly in every way, but she needed
something . . . a softening . . . an acceptance of her own
vulnerability, before she could really rise to the top.
'I've told you before about taking work home,' he
scolded. 'I thought you left early on Friday to go and
visit your aunt.'

'That was Friday,' she pointed out. 'It still left
Saturday and Sunday. And anway, when else am I
supposed to study all these notes and write these
reports?'

He gave up. 'You'll come over to Sunday lunch with us
next week, won't you, eh? Muriel hasn't seen you for ages,
and I know the children would love to as well. I believe
Julia and her brood will be there. What about it, Anna?'

Daniel's oldest daughter was married and had
presented him with two small grandchildren, whom he
adored. Anna smiled gratefully. 'I certainly will.
Thanks.'

'Good, good. Now . . .' He consulted his watch.
'You're not here to chat. Our first customers will be
here any time. You're here to talk to me about the fact
that the Tyrell case has raised its complex head in your
list again, eh?' Straight to the point, as usual.

'Correct. Daniel . . .' She leaned forwards earnestly,
both elbows on his desk, hands linked under chin as she
gazed directly at him. 'Do I have to take it back? It's
been a year or more, you know, and I don't see why . . .
I know how busy you are, and anyway it may not be
your sort of case; but couldn't Gill? She's so good with
adolescent boys,' she pleaded convincingly. 'She'd do it
much better than me.'

'Two things, Anna.' He was mild, sympathetic—but very firm. 'Firstly, this is not a case for simple counselling. If it were, I'd have given it to Gill in the first place. Christopher Tyrell is in a bad way. He needs trained, expert professional help.'

'He was in a bad way a year ago,' Anna observed caustically. 'If I'd been allowed to see it through, I could have had him settling down by now.'

'Yes, well ... unfortunately we don't have the ultimate jurisdiction over our clients' parents or guardians,' Daniel reminded her. 'I dare say you could have achieved your usual miracle, but he wasn't bad enough to justify a court order going against the elder brother ... and now it seems things have taken a turn for the worse.'

'So, they come running back to us.' Anna was deeply sardonic. 'What's the matter, anyway? Is he still truanting, or is there something else?'

'Oh yes, he never stopped refusing school. He's passed school leaving age now, so it isn't even illegal. But he stayed away all year, never even took a single O-level or CSE. No, it's not that. He's in trouble with the law. Cannabis.'

So Pam had been right in her melodramatic suspicion. 'Smoking, possessing or pushing?'

'Being in possession of. I gather it was at a party. But he was as high as a kite that time, according to police reports, and freely admits he's been using the drug, and probably others too, for some time. Now, the brother seems to have finally agreed that the boy needs treatment and help, which is something after his less than constructive attitude a year ago.'

'I should say it is,' endorsed Anna vehemently.

'Which brings me to the second reason I want you to take this case on again. I could send them to another Unit, or even one of the big clinics ... but in my opinion, Anna, you're the person who'd do it best. And,' he fixed her with those gimlet grey eyes, behind the thick lenses, 'what's more, you ought to face up to your own challenge in connection with it.'

Her stomach tightened into a knot. What the hell was he getting at now? She lifted her chin defiantly. 'What do you mean, Daniel? I know I got angry with the man, but you must admit he asked for it. He was so obstructive, he made my work impossible.'

'It wasn't just that, though, was it? The way the two of you clashed, it was almost as if it was *because* of you he took Christopher away! I could feel the sparks, hear the fireworks from in here. Now's your chance to put him right—and surely, confront a crisis which was yours almost as much as Christopher's?'

'Are you telling me you think I should follow this through for my *own* sake?' Anna could hardly believe her ears. Daniel may be wise and shrewd, but really— this was verging on the ridiculous!

'In a way, yes. I haven't forgotten how upset you were a year ago when it hit you. Well, here's a heaven-sent opportunity to resolve an unfinished conflict.'

'But, Daniel . . .' She leaned back in her chair, stunned by this bombshell. Then she grinned, taking refuge behind humour, which was one of her tricks. 'Well, you're the psychiatrist around here. I'll have to take your word for it. I'll do my best.' She stood up, neatly evading any further burrowing on his part. She knew she was doing it, and so did he; but at least the seeds of his point had been sown. 'I'll study the file at lunchtime. Will Big Brother be coming in this time, do you know?' She looked Daniel straight in the eye, her expression blank.

'I've no idea.' A small smile played about one corner of his mouth. 'Now, don't go without lunch, Anna. Get Pam to bring you some rolls from the Greek shop or something if you're not going out. And good luck; remember I'm here if you need support, moral or otherwise. When you think about it, I'm sure you'd hate yourself if you backed out of a challenge. Any challenge,' he added inscrutably.

'Oh, I'm sure I would.' Anna snapped her briefcase shut, and sent him another breezy grin. Turning at the door, she said 'Thanks,' before opening it.

Daniel's rich booming chuckle echoed into the corridor after her. 'For nothing, eh?' he called after her. Pulling a face to herself—amused exasperation—she closed the door and walked on up to her own consulting room. She had several files to read, and her first client would be waiting. Christopher Tyrell and his autocratic brother Neil were not the only pebbles on the beach. She had a whole day of other unfortunate young people to deal with before it was their turn.

'Therapy for the therapist now, is it?' she muttered to herself as she studied the first two cases of the day, refreshing her memory about the details. A little later she buzzed Pam on the internal 'phone, adopting her most crisp, brusque tone. 'Okay, Pam. I'm ready for Timothy now, if he's there.'

'Right, Anna.' Pam's voice was its usual mixture of affection and deference. There was nothing abnormal about this Monday. She would conduct her sessions, keep everything in its proper perspective, as she always did. Nothing could threaten her that way.

If Anna had not trained herself to push every personal consideration right to the back of her mind, concentrating all her intellectual energies on the cases in hand, she would never have managed her problem clients as skilfully and calmly as she did. It was no use calling yourself a Child Psychologist, that most demanding and responsible of vocations, if you couldn't discipline yourself. How could you help or heal other minds if your own was not well under control?

This morning, however, it wasn't easy. The latest development, and Daniel's enigmatic comments about it, niggled at the back of her thoughts as she watched and listened, questioned and encouraged her small clients, outwardly displaying all her normal patient insight. But there was no way she was going to let her other cases suffer just because she was a little on edge about the last one of the day.

At lunchtime she obeyed Daniel's instructions and asked Pam to buy her two of the fresh cheese rolls, sprinkled with sesame seeds, which went like hot cakes from the Greek grocer round the corner every midday. Then she made herself a cup of coffee in the tiny common room, where there were facilities for hot drinks and snacks, and shut herself in her own room to think and to peruse the Tyrell file. It was vital to catch up on every detail of the boy's latest problems. She must know exactly what she was up against.

Flicking over the pages, she reminded herself of what the case had originally been about. A year ago, Christopher had been a gangling, gawky lad of fifteen, tall for his age, bony, with lank fair hair falling into sullen blue eyes, and the usual endowment of greasy skin and adolescent spots. But somewhere beneath that unattractive, awkward exterior, Anna had sensed an appealing, endearing creature struggling to escape and be appreciated.

He had been referred after persistently truanting from school for months on end, then breaking down completely. He had, it seemed, retired into a private cocoon. It was a conscious decision not to face the world any more. According to reports from welfare officers and the family doctor, he had sat in a corner of his own room, refusing to leave it, refusing to talk, eating very little, rejecting all approaches. He was never violent or even aggressive; just deeply withdrawn and—as Anna instantly recognised—seriously clinically depressed.

During their first session Anna had been able to get very little out of the boy apart from surly grunts. He had been plucked from the safety of his home, brought here to this alien place to be questioned by a totally strange woman. She could not really blame him for his lack of co-operation. Before she could achieve anything she had to win his trust, and that might take quite a while in itself.

Afterwards she had a brief chat with the social workers who had brought him, probing behind the dry words of their report to get at the realities beneath. 'I don't get the impression he's materially deprived,' she had remarked, glancing at the notes.

'Oh no,' Helen had agreed. 'He's got a lovely home; there's no shortage of money.'

'It's all really comfortable,' Fiona had echoed. 'I mean, he's got lots of—you know—things, but it's just too quiet and tidy to be cosy, if you know what I mean. At least, that's the feeling I get from him, and his room,' she added hastily.

'We haven't had a proper look at the house yet,' Helen explained. 'Or met the older brother who lives with him. We've got to do that, now he's coming here.'

Anna was still reading through the notes. 'Yes, he was brought up by this brother, wasn't he? What happened to their parents, do you know?'

Fiona shook her head. 'Not sure—some kind of accident, we think, but we can't ask too much or he gets more upset than ever. And we haven't interviewed the brother because he's been away recently. Has to travel for his job, or something.'

'Away?' Anna was surprised, raising her head to stare at them. 'Who looks after Christopher then?'

'Oh, he's not neglected or anything like that. There's a housekeeper, seems kind and competent enough, and when he was young there were *au pairs* and all that, but . . .'

'But that's no substitute for a parent or someone really involved.' Anna nodded slowly. 'I see; poor little chap. No wonder he's been traumatised. I wonder why it's suddenly erupted now . . .?' she mused, half to herself. 'We've got a job on our hands with this one,' she reflected, sensing that glow of anticipation which always marked the start of a new challenge. 'But we'll do our best. Now.' She became brisk. 'What about this brother? You don't know him yet, but he's the legal guardian, is that right? Must be a lot older than Christopher? Are they really brothers, not half-brothers or something like that?'

'Oh yes,' Helen assured her. 'They're certainly brothers, as far as we know. He was born when their mother was very young, obviously, and—let me see— twenty-five when the parents died, so he'll be in his thirties by now. There's seventeen years between them. I think the family doctor reported that the parents spent years trying for another child, and had all but given up hope when Chris arrived on the scene.'

'Must have been a shock to everyone,' observed Fiona.

'Not least the older brother himself.' Anna nodded again, understanding of the situation taking shape in her mind. 'Looks like an interesting conflict of rivalries and jealousies we'll be getting into here, possibly in both directions. So, apart from the fact that he must have given his consent for Christopher to be here at all, you don't know what the brother's general attitude to all this is?'

'Not really. We had to persuade Chris to come here today, but he's so limp, he didn't really put up a fight,' Helen said.

'No.' Anna was silent for a moment as she contemplated the plight of yet another unhappy child. 'Well, please make sure I get to meet this brother when he condescends to return among us.'

At the second session, three days later, there was a slight but marked improvement. Christopher appeared to have decided that any interest was better than none, and a few of his grunts took on the shape of words under Anna's subtle encouragement. Only a few, and not very helpful words, but it was a step in the right direction. Anna felt optimistic and excited.

And then, at the third session the next week, the whole enterprise changed radically. Instead of turning up in the social worker's battered old Austin, Christopher stepped out from the passenger seat of a smoothly polished Rover. Instead of being escorted into the consulting room by Helen or Fiona, he skulked—literally—in the shadow of someone totally different.

For one thing, his new companion was male. About Christopher's height, but much broader, with the width of shoulder and chest the boy had yet to grow into. Similarly long legs, encased in similarly tight jeans, were about the full extent of the resemblance, apart from an inevitable family likeness about the face. Where the boy was scruffy, unkempt and droopy, the man was sharp, clean-cut and confident. Where the boy's hair hung apologetically over his thin sad face, the man's sprang energetically around forceful, square features and a positive expression.

Christopher's eyes were a pale, defeated blue, his complexion washed out. The man's were also blue, but quick and piercing; his skin tough, with a tan certainly not picked up in an English spring. The boy's hair was a dirty blond; the man's genuinely, strikingly fair, curling on to a high wide brow and down over the collar of his open-necked cotton shirt.

Christopher Tyrell's older brother had arrived.

Anna knew he was there, after a warning buzz on the intercom from Pam, and she stood up to greet them as they entered, ready with her warmest smile. This was a big moment in the case. Involving the parents and guardians was as important as the sessions with the children. She had been eager to meet this man, and now she held out a hand to him as he came through the door, striding ahead of his younger brother who loped in his wake with an air of resignation.

Anna's professional instincts were stirred into realisation of a basic truth as she saw them together: Christopher's problems may have begun with the loss of his parents, but they had undoubtedly been compounded in subsequent years—and here was the root of them, confronting her now, an expression of ironic curiosity plastered all over his intelligent, attractive face. On top of all those other traumas, the boy was having to contend with a classic case of sibling rivalry, and no wonder. The adult Neil was everything the adolescent Christopher was not: successful, mature, composed. Even at twenty-five, Neil had probably already achieved a good deal of the poise and charisma he carried about now with him like a natural second skin. Over the intervening years these had grown and developed, and young Christopher's sense of loss had been increased by a sense of failure. How could he ever

hope to emulate his big brother, who also had to be
father and mother rolled into one? Anna's heart went
out to him as her determination to help him hardened.

'Miss—Coleman?' The smile was sincere and direct,
and yet somehow it mocked, narrowing the eyes,
bringing lines to their corners; lengthening the long
mouth and revealing white, slightly overlapping, teeth.
The voice was as deep and firm as Christopher's was
reedy and uncertain. The hand which shook hers was
warm, dry and enveloping.

She drew hers away at once, gesturing to them both
to sit down, her smile fading. '*Dr* Coleman, yes. How
do you do, Mr Tyrell.'

His eyebrows were almost as fair as the hair they now
disappeared into. 'I do beg your pardon. I had no idea
you were medically qualified. You scarcely appear
mature enough to have collected such a string of
accomplishments.' It was a backhanded compliment,
she knew perfectly well, as she schooled herself not to
become flustered under his all-encompassing inspection.

'I am not medically qualified,' she explained coolly.
'When I use the title Doctor, it's because I have a PhD.
I have a degree in Sociology, a Doctorate in Social
Psychology and a Diploma in Clinical Psychology.'

'Very impressive,' he drawled, leaning back in his
chair and stretching his long legs in front of him. Then
he yawned, making it plain that academic distinctions
left him fairly cold; and making it plainer to Anna's
eagle eye that he had a chip on his own shoulder several
feet wide when it came to this subject.

'My senior colleague, Dr Davidson, is a psychiatrist,'
she went on to inform him, 'and therefore a doctor of
medicine as well. But I'm not.'

'Fair enough.' He leaned forward now, his gaze
intense on her face. 'I didn't come here to discuss the
letters after your names,' he announced tersely. 'I came
to see what you're up to with my kid brother here.' He
gestured to Christopher, without looking at him. The
boy sat quietly, staring straight ahead.

'What we're up to?' Anna echoed, struggling to keep

a growing hostility out of her tone. This man's attitude
was only too clear. Not only was he responsible for a
good deal of his brother's trouble; he was going the
right way about causing some more here, too. 'What
we're up to,' she emphasised the words with delicate
disapproval, 'is endeavouring to help him through a
difficult period, and find out what's made it so difficult.
That's all.' She disliked talking about one of her clients
in front of them, and forcibly pulled the conversation to
a more general level. 'Now, Mr Tyrell, would you like
to tell me a bit more about yourself—your job, for
instance? What do you and Christopher like to do in
your spare time? Where do you . . .'

But Neil Tyrell had risen to his feet, his face clouded
with anger. 'I didn't come here to make small talk
either,' he grated. 'I want to know how you intend to
help Chris—if, that is, you have any idea. It seems to
me that all this talk gets people nowhere. Action is
what's called for.'

Anna was standing now, too, confronting him across
the desk. Only the boy remained sitting where he was,
impassive, as if all this concerned someone else. 'And
what kind of action did you have in mind, Mr Tyrell?'
she enquired coldly.

He shrugged, thrusting expressive hands into his
pockets. 'That's your department, flower.' The mock
respect had fled out of the window. Clearly, Neil Tyrell
was not a man to bow before superior knowledge or
experience, any more than qualifications. 'That's what
we're here to establish. Isn't it?' He gazed at her
insolently.

Gripping the edge of her desk, Anna channelled her
irritation into firmness. 'Look, Mr Tyrell, we need your
help and co-operation if we're going to help your
brother. His problems are closely connected with you.
He's . . .'

'His problems?' The man was glaring at her openly
now. 'Chris hasn't got any problems!' Unaccountably, he
had grown even angrier. 'Okay, so we lost our parents.
Don't forget they were my parents as well as his.'

*And you'd had them all to yourself for—what was it?—
seventeen years, before small brother came on the scene
and spoiled things*, Anna's professional mind retorted in
her head. But she held her peace. This was no moment
to start analysing him.

'I've done my best for him,' Neil was ranting. 'He's
never lacked for a thing. What he needs to do is pull
himself together and stop creating such a childish fuss.
Get on with life, as we all have to do.'

She stared at him blankly for several seconds, almost
unable to believe her ears. Surely he wasn't serious?
Childish fuss? Was that how he saw his brother's
terrible depression? How could he be so blind, stupid
. . . heartless? She was filled with rage against him, and
with pity for the boy, who still sat in the chair near
them—wordless, motionless, expressionless. Here was a
complex case, something she really could get her teeth
into, given half a chance!

But that would take the full co-operation of this
alarming man, so she bit back the cutting responses she
could feel pushing their way out, and pulled out all the
tactful stops. 'Look,' she suggested, all sweet reason,
'this is very bad for Christopher. Why don't we start
from the beginning again?' She turned to the boy.
'Christopher, would you please go along to the waiting
room for a few minutes? We'll call you back very soon,
okay?'

Christopher got up without a word and sloped out
with every sign of relief. Anna buzzed through to Pam,
alerting her to his arrival and telling her to make sure he
stayed put and didn't disappear. Then she turned back
to his brother, her expression a study in calm
persuasion. 'Now, Mr Tyrell, you do want to help him,
don't you?'

He was scrutinising her closely now, arms folded,
anger apparently subsided. 'Oh sure, *Dr* Coleman. But
it seems to me the best person to help Chris is Chris.
Hasn't he got any willpower? He used to be a bright,
happy kid, until a few weeks back. I'm sure it wasn't
my fault, whatever went wrong. And it sure as hell

wasn't yours,' he added sarcastically. 'So what do *you* propose to do for him?'

The clear challenge was issued in a tone of pure cynicism. One fact stood out a mile: Neil Tyrell had no faith at all in the powers of psychologists, psychiatrists, therapists, counsellors. 'First,' Anna said, 'we have to get him to talk.'

'Talk!' His lips curled scathingly around the useless word. 'Always talk!'

'Okay then—what do you suggest?' she parried, quietly.

'Action. Isn't there something he can take, to get him over this patch?'

'Medication?' Her brows were perfect arches, a study in polite distaste. 'You want us to feed your own brother tranquillisers? Isn't he subdued enough for you already?'

'God no, of course I didn't mean that ... but surely, anti-depressants ...? For a short time, till he's over the worst ...?' He watched her: wary, laconic.

'We use medication only as a last resort, not at the first whiff of trouble,' she explained stiffly. 'I have no doubts that we can help Christopher by other means. It might take us a while, but after all that's what we're here for. And if we're to achieve anything, Mr Tyrell, we're going to need your willing assistance, not just your reluctant permission.' Her hazel eyes never once left his face as she said it.

'My willing assistance, no less?' Neil was satirical now, his own deep blue eyes skitting across her earnest countenance and down over her body. Suddenly the desk between them seemed a flimsy barrier, and Anna looked down at it, colouring. 'And exactly what form does this willing assistance have to take?' he wondered lightly.

'Just your active encouragement, for now. Make sure he gets here when we want him. Come with him if necessary. Do your best to make him see it's for his sake.'

He paused, still studying her. Then he grunted.

'Okay, okay. But I still think you're all making mountains out of molehills.' Bitterness sharpened his features, just briefly. 'When I was his age, if you didn't toe the line you were bloody well beaten till you did.'

'That happened to you?' She stared at him in disbelief.

'Not at home. I was at boarding school. The full public school bit, you know. Young Chris never had to go through all that lot. He doesn't know when he's well off.'

Anna regarded him thoughtfully. Brief snatches, tantalising glimpses into this man's character were all she had seen, but it was enough to make several things clearer about his brother. 'We'll keep you in touch about how it's going,' she promised. 'And a bit later, we may ask you to come in with him for a few sessions. It can be extremely important. It's called Family Therapy.'

'Oh, great.' From his expression, he had no intention of participating in any such process. 'Happy Families, eh? Cosy.'

Anna hardly bothered to stifle her grin. She shook her head, sitting down again behind her desk. 'We do our best to make it relaxed, yes,' she said, deliberately ignoring his sarcasm. 'Now, I've only got half Christopher's session left, so if you could go through and send him back along, we can get on with it.'

Her cool attitude clearly infuriated him. His eyes narrowed. 'So, that's it, then? Dismissed? Patted on the head and sent packing?'

'I didn't put it quite like that,' she protested. 'But I'm very busy.'

He regarded her fiercely for several seconds, then swung on his heel and strode to the door. 'Very well, Dr Coleman. Your wish is my command. I shall return baby brother into your tender mercies and leave you to practise your voodoo on him.'

Anna stared after him, wondering which of the two brothers was the more confused and in need of help. At the same time, on quite another level, she was struggling to still various strange flutterings and churnings his presence seemed to have started up in her. All difficult interviews had that effect, she told herself; but Neil Tyrell's potent hostility had breached defences she hardly even knew she had. At least, she could only suppose it was his hostility, and the matching defiance he sparked off in her. If there was something else, some hidden ingredient she had never met, mixed in with their mutual reaction, she preferred to leave it well hidden. She had enough to do, probing into the minds of her patients, without delving too deeply into her own responses.

The ensuing session with Christopher was predictably disappointing. Not surprisingly, the conversation he'd witnessed between them plunged him even further into verbal paralysis. Anna cursed herself for not seeing his brother alone at the start.

But the following week she had two further sessions with him which really seemed to be getting somewhere. He began to open out, talk about his early memories of his parents and his brother. Anna allowed herself to feel a little more hopeful and positive about the case. If she could bide her time, it might work out.

But she was destined for disappointment. The case never had the chance to work out. On the Monday there was a letter from Neil Tyrell, stating boldly that in his opinion the sessions were upsetting his brother and making him worse. He did not wish the boy to be forced into recalling a part of his life which could only hurt him. He thanked the Child Guidance Unit for their interest, but assured them he would deal with the situation in his own way from then on. It was, he pointed out, still his legal responsibility to care for his brother, and this he fully intended to do. And that was that.

There was nothing they could do except notify the Social Services Department and check that they were still keeping an eye on the case. It was a severe blow to Anna's professional pride and integrity. At a more personal level, she was concerned for Christopher himself: how would the uncompromising Neil 'deal with' his brother? Whatever methods he chose, she was quite sure the iron fist would not be clothed in a velvet glove.

She confided these fears when she reported the whole confrontation afterwards to Daniel Davidson. 'How can *anyone* be so stupid and short-sighted?' she moaned, for the third time. 'Doesn't he *care* about his brother?'

'In his own way, I'm sure he does,' Daniel had reassured her in his gentle manner. 'I've got a feeling he might have put on a lot of that heavy talk for your benefit.'

'Mine? Why should he want to do that?' Anna was genuinely puzzled.

'Can't you work it out? A woman in that role: the expert in charge of his brother's case, probing into all his possible weaknesses and lapses? From the way you describe him, a chap like Neil Tyrell wouldn't care for that one bit.'

'I never thought of that.' It was a deeply unsettling notion, and she didn't like it at all. 'Why can't people forget what sex we are and just let us do the work?'

'Why indeed?' Daniel was deadly serious, but his eyes twinkled. 'Gets in all over the place, doesn't it, this wicked sex business?' He shook his head. 'Not to worry, Anna. It's out of our hands, for the moment.'

And so it had been: the file shelved, the case discontinued—until today. Now the law had stepped in, and Neil had been forced to allow his brother to receive the outside help he had so high-handedly rejected a year ago. Anna had been proved right. The man could not manage the boy's problems on his own. Things had got worse, and now he was in trouble with the police. Just another statistic in the terrible story of young people and drug abuse.

Brooding over the Tyrell file, which had been taken out and dusted off, she shook her head grimly. She was about to face Christopher again any minute, and more than likely his brother, too. Daniel was nearer the mark than she had cared to admit to his face: this was going to be a test, and not just at the professional level. It had been her case then, and it was still her case now. The months had not dulled that sense of heightened awareness she had felt at the start of it. Even if she had succeeded in banishing Neil Tyrell to the outer edge of her memory, she had never for a moment forgotten him altogether. And now he was back in her in-tray; in her life, along with all his brother's problems. She must welcome the opportunity to renew an intriguing professional challenge. Anna was not one to flinch from a task, and now she braced herself, quelling those nagging inner voices of trepidation as she welcomed it.

CHAPTER TWO

CHRISTOPHER duly arrived, fussed over anxiously by the two social workers as if they expected him to collapse into a heap between them. Anna was shocked by the deterioration in his appearance. Where before he had been skinny and withdrawn, now he looked emaciated, his eyes oddly glazed, his hands hanging loosely at his sides.

'I presume someone'll be here to see he gets home safely afterwards?' she drew them briefly aside to ask, once the boy was installed in her consulting room.

'One of us will be here,' Helen promised. 'He's not fit to travel on his own.'

Anna hesitated, one hand on the door handle, strangely reluctant to put the next question. 'I suppose Big Brother might deign to honour us with his presence eventually? I'll have to see him again if I'm to get anywhere with all this.'

'He's abroad at the moment,' Fiona explained. 'I expect he'll be in touch when he gets back.' The two girls exchanged expressive glances: obviously they had covered this ground before and had their own opinions about Neil Tyrell, formulated during this past year of dealing with the problems of his young brother.

'Abroad?' Anna's brows lifted. 'Must be important, to take him away just now.'

'He came to the court hearing. After he heard that Christopher was remanded for psychiatric reports, he scooted off. He does that a lot these days: more than ever.'

'It's to do with his work,' Helen elaborated, when Anna looked even more puzzled.

'Why—what does he do, exactly?' Anna glanced at her watch; she must not leave Christopher unattended in the room much longer, but this was an important piece of data.

Helen and Fiona were gazing at her in round-eyed amazement. 'Don't you *know*?'

'No.' Anna looked from one to the other. 'Should I have heard of him?'

'He's in television. He's really well-known—makes films,' Helen told her.

In spite of herself, Anna was intrigued. 'Is he an actor, then?'

'Oh no. He's on the directing side, or producing, or whatever you call it. He's brilliant!' Helen became enthusiastic, her voice rising above its former hushed, tactful whisper as she forgot the presence of the boy on the other side of the door. 'You must have seen that documentary about the Chinese commune, and the one about the factory workers in Tokyo? And that thing set behind the scenes of a huge orchestra . . .'

The less volatile Fiona laid a finger on her lips, but she was grinning at her colleague. 'He's hot on conservation issues, too,' she added. 'Stuff on species threatened with extinction, that kind of thing. Marvellous camera work.'

'I see.' Their eulogy on the man came as something of a shock to Anna, whose face and tone assumed an unusual stiffness. 'I had no idea we were up against a minor celebrity. Might explain a few of their psychological problems. And you say he goes away a lot—even more than he used to before?'

'Increasingly, these last few months. I suppose he's just getting more high-powered and in greater demand all the time,' Fiona conjectured.

'Do you ever raise the subject with him?' Anna enquired thoughtfully.

'Not really.' They smiled ruefully at each other. 'He's a difficult man, tends to fly off the handle if you seem to be finding fault. We don't see much of him.'

'Difficult,' Helen endorsed, a slight glint in her blue eyes. 'But dishy.'

Anna grunted. 'Well, I'd better get in there or our friend will doze off in his chair.'

She had hardly expected to get far with Christopher today, but she had seldom encountered quite such a brick wall. He was inert, totally internalised, oblivious to her every attempt to draw him out. In the past year he had sunk deep into depression and detachment, and dabbling in drugs had only intensified his already bemused state.

She watched his lanky frame slouch out at the end of the session. Then she sat at her desk for a long time, drained and tense, making notes and re-reading the file until she knew it by heart. It was late when she left the clinic, still brooding; and for the next two days, as she went about the routine of seeing her other clients, Christopher Tyrell was always somewhere at the fringes of her consciousness. He seemed to have taken root, threatening her precious objectivity in a way she had always sworn to avoid.

He was due again on Thursday. When she arrived that morning and picked up her file of folders from the tray, Pam drew her attention to a note pinned to the Tyrell file. 'He 'phoned ten minutes ago,' she declared helpfully.

'He? Who?' Anna frowned as she peered at the note. 'Ah—I see.'

'Mr Tyrell, Senior. The social workers said you wanted to see him, so I've made an appointment.'

Anna studied her own reaction to this piece of news. She could hardly pretend to herself that it came as a shock: after all, she had ordered his presence at the sessions. But now that it was an immediate reality, the prospect of confronting the man again flooded her with a quality and quantity of nervous apprehension which appalled her. This was disastrous! She valued her cool detachment above all things, and such instant, instinctive emotional responses were well beyond her permitted scale. She fought to regain complete control of herself, and some of her tension transferred itself in Pam's direction before she had time to prevent it.

'When?' she snapped. 'It'll be no use if Christopher's

there too, you know, Pam. We'd need a good hour; and we'd need it alone,' she pointed out tetchily.

Pam looked up from the papers she was busy shuffling, her expression faintly surprised. 'Of course! I should know that by now, Anna. I fitted him into your last free slot today. You've got Christopher this morning, right? So I thought you could see Mr Tyrell this afternoon—you didn't have a client at four—then you'd have a bit more to base the interview on.'

Anna was already regretting her momentary lapse into irritation. It had been aimed at herself, after all; it wasn't fair to take it out on the efficient Pam. 'Absolutely right, as always, Pam—eminently sensible. What would we do without you?' She grinned as she pushed the swing door open with her shoulder, both arms full of the perennial overflowing briefcase. 'Let's hope I have something more positive to report when I do see him,' she muttered, half to herself, as she set off down the corridor.

But it was a fond hope. There was a change, but you could hardly call it an improvement. This time Christopher seemed more agitated and less remote, his fingers twisting themselves together in writhing knots, his abstracted gaze occasionally flickering round the room, pierced suddenly from within by some very real pang of emotion—fear, perhaps, or anger, or both. Watching him carefully, Anna reminded herself that this boy was no fool. Before his breakdown he had been exceptionally clever and sociable at school. All that brightness must be there still, locked away somewhere behind the unhappy mask. If only she could get him to respond, just a little! There had to be a basis, however flimsy, from which to begin even the simplest analysis. If he refused to communicate even in grunts, how could she find out what she was up against or decide where to go next?

Once again she was exhausted when she saw him off, but a lunchtime chat with Daniel and Gill proved helpful. Reinforced by their support, she felt ready to face the other half of the Tyrell challenge.

If Christopher had altered for the worse in the last twelve months, his brother certainly had not. He strode into Anna's room at four o'clock precisely, immediately dominating it just as he had before. She shot him a quick cool glance: his outward image was much as she clearly—if unwillingly—recalled it, especially that air of irony about the sharp blue eyes, veiling, as she knew, a suppressed animosity. Superficially he was supremely self-contained and confident, though wary; but Anna's trained instincts warned her that at a deeper level he seethed with arrogant resentment.

Time might have frozen as they faced each other from exactly the same positions as a year ago. Neil Tyrell stood with feet planted firmly apart, hands in the pockets of his short jacket; Anna sat behind the safe fortress of her desk, allowing her lucid hazel eyes to rest thoughtfully on his face. This time she did not stand up or offer him her hand. Instead she nodded calmly in his direction, her mouth curving into the merest suggestion of a smile, and she waved her hand at the chair opposite her. 'So, Mr Tyrell, we meet again. Won't you sit down?'

If he was spoiling for a fight, her bland politeness did nothing to mollify him. He stayed where he was, staring down at her while she bent her glossy dark head and went on writing her notes. Then his long mouth quirked into a sardonic grin and he lowered himself gracefully into the proffered armchair.

'Won't keep you a moment,' she assured him without lifting her head.

'My time is yours, Dr Coleman.' His deadpan courtesy more than matched hers, as he leaned comfortably back in the chair to study her—or as much as he could see of her—with undisguised approval. 'I'm at your disposal; that's why I came. I'll happily sit here and enjoy the view.'

She glanced up then, puzzled, because the only view from her consulting room window was of the dull grey house next door. Too late, she realised his meaning— and understood that for a man like this, no form of attack would be taboo, no holds would be barred. He was now making this abundantly clear as his insolent gaze lingered meditatively over her shapely legs and ankles, clad today in tights under a pleated skirt and crossed neatly, but quite visibly, under her desk.

Furious with herself for falling into his trap, she concentrated on her notes, acutely aware of his eyes following the contours of her calves, feeling their touch as surely as if he was stroking her bare skin with his fingertips. He had no need for a degree in Psychology; an unerring male intuition told him exactly where her only vulnerability lay. Intellectually, professionally, Anna was equal to anything or anyone. Physically, sexually, she was as uncertain and unawakened as a child. Usually the strength managed to control and eclipse the weakness, but once in a while a person came along who could effortlessly undermine that control— and it was already painfully clear that Neil Tyrell was one of those people. Her deepest instinct now was to turn and run in the opposite direction before it was too late (though too late for what exactly, she was too cowardly even to wonder). But Anna was expert at ignoring her deepest instincts, or at least relegating them to barely discernible mutterings, and years of relentless practice came into play now.

Sedately, taking her time, she finished writing and then deliberately put her pen down and raised her head to look at him. He sat with arms folded across his broad chest, still contemplating her with wry appreciation. A shaft of spring sunlight found its way through the window and slanted across him, picking out a bright streak, almost silver, in the fair vitality of his hair.

'Now then, Mr Tyrell. I'm grateful to you for coming. I won't say I'm surprised to see you again, but I'm very sorry it had to be in such circumstances.'

'*You told me so*, is that it?' he mocked. 'No doubt you're thinking, Dr Coleman, only you're too well-bred to say so, that this is all my bloody fault, and if I'd let Chris go on coming here in the first place it wouldn't be necessary.'

It was a pretty accurate assessment, and Anna found herself smiling slightly. 'Naturally we were extremely dismayed when you decided to withdraw your brother last year, just as we thought we were making some progress . . .'

'Oh, you thought that, did you?' His true hostility showed itself briefly. 'Well, I begged to differ. In my opinion it could do nothing but harm, making the poor guy relive all those early memories, digging out his feelings about our parents and all that. He came home in a terrible state. He spent half the night in tears!' he exploded, as if this was the ultimate disaster.

'Do nothing but harm to whom?' Anna demanded, beginning to understand his attitude.

'To Chris, of course. Who did you think I meant?' he growled, clearly not liking her implication. 'He was really—I mean *really*—turned inside out.'

Anna leaned forward in her eagerness to explain the point to him. 'But that was just what we were trying to achieve! If he didn't go through all that, our methods wouldn't be working. If only you'd given me a chance to confide in you and explain a bit more at the time . . .' Conquering a rising impatience, she continued, 'Mr Tyrell, Christopher has some terrible, deep-seated anger and sorrow to shift. The only way we can help him is to—dig it out, as you put it. Force him to get it all on the outside.'

'Like coughing up poison,' Neil observed with profound cynicism.

But Anna was undaunted by his sarcasm. 'Exactly—you've got it!' She leaned on the desk now, eyes shining. 'He'll never be well until he's got past it. We can help him do that; at least, we thought we could then.' Her tone hardened. 'It might be a lot more difficult now, but we'll try.'

'You mean, it's not going too well?'

'So far I've had two sessions with him, and I have to tell you I'm not optimistic.'

His expression barely twitched, but Anna was well aware of the pain this flat statement caused him. 'All this—anger and sorrow.' Against his own inclination, he was making an effort. 'Are you saying it's—left over from when our parents got killed?'

'I am saying that, yes. That was the start of it, at least, I imagine.' She was quiet now, watching him closely.

His gaze had softened and turned inwards, tearing itself away from her to wander about the room as his attention focused on to a long-buried past. 'He was really brave, when it happened,' he mused, as if thinking aloud. 'Upset and bewildered of course, but tough. I was proud of him. He was only eight, you know.'

'I know,' Anna assured him softly, biding her time now, metaphorically crossing her fingers as he relaxed and opened up a little.

'He turned to me for protection. There were grandparents, aunts, people like that—but he wanted to be with me. It seemed obvious. We belonged together. I gave him everything he wanted and needed. Everything was fine, until—oh, I don't know—eighteen months ago?' His eyes blazed suddenly, fiercely questioning. 'Why, Dr Coleman? What went wrong?'

Anna detected guilt and self-doubt lurking behind all that defensive aggression. Perhaps they were beginning to make some headway; but she remained outwardly impassive. 'It wasn't your fault,' she told him carefully. 'He'd been storing it all up for years. It was bound to break through sometime. Did anything happen just before that time,' she wondered mildly, 'which might have triggered off such a major change in him?'

'Nothing at all,' Neil replied at once. 'I told you, he seemed fine, and then . . .'

'You have to go away quite a bit, don't you, as part of your work?' she interrupted with a bland enquiry, following a hunch.

'Sure. I'm a media-man,' he reminded her tersely. 'I can't very well put films together without being on the spot, can I?'

'I did hear that you worked in television.' Anna was

cautious, retaining her control over the situation. 'I don't have one myself—I prefer radio. Leaves me free to do something else more constructive at the same time.'

He regarded her with renewed interest. 'Beneath your dignity, eh, the old one-eyed monster? Mindless entertainment for the mindless masses?'

She disregarded his sarcasm again. 'Not at all. We all have our different ways of relaxing,' she retorted coolly. 'I was simply making the point that you're bound to have to travel, as part of the job.'

'Yes, I do. More and more. So what? Chris is always well looked after,' he snapped, rising to her implied criticism. 'He's always had everything he needs.'

'How far do you have to go?' Anna pressed, still pursuing her train of thought. 'And how long do you stay away?'

He stared at her for a moment, then shrugged. 'I used to try and keep the trips short, but a couple of years back I started working freelance, and that meant spending a fair bit of time in some exotic locations: China, Japan, Israel . . .'

'A couple of years ago?' Anna deliberately re-emphasised his own point.

Neil's blue eyes darkened as he picked up her drift. 'You mean, Chris's troubles started when I began to spend longer away from home and travelled further away?'

Anna shrugged. 'It's a possibility, isn't it? He can't be very secure, after all. That might have been the last straw. You're all he's got. At least you were usually around, or if you weren't it was only for a few days— but suddenly you started deserting him for weeks at a time, taking off for the other side of the world without him, leaving him alone to cope. You might have thought he was tough,' she told him, her tone hardening as she determined not to let him down lightly, 'but no child's as tough as that. I don't suppose,' she rammed the point home, 'you ever really encouraged him to grieve when your parents died, to make a fuss?' His face grew pale but he remained silent. 'Did you? Anna persisted.

Neil shook his head, following her reasoning with a grudging attention. 'I told you,' he muttered, 'I was proud of him, not breaking down at the time . . .'

'Keeping a stiff upper lip?' Anna could not be bothered to conceal the irony in her reaction. 'And I dare say you did quite a bit of that yourself, didn't you?'

Stung, he took refuge in antagonism again. 'Bear in mind, petal, I was a man of twenty-five at the time, not a snivelling youth wet behind the ears.'

'But Christopher was just a little boy,' she pointed out, unable to keep the disapproval from her tone. 'And had a profound need to let out his grief, share his loss with you. There's more to—what did you call it?— protection, than simply providing material comforts and enough to eat,' she reminded him acidly. 'What's more,' she went on, when he failed to respond, 'there's nothing shameful about showing emotions, you know, at any age.'

'The way I was brought up there was.' He was glaring down at his hands, spread palms downwards on his knees. For a fleeting instant she spotted an echo of his younger brother in the droop of the jaw, the sullen, almost petulant, set of the lips. 'Emotional outbursts aren't my scene. I wouldn't know how to handle them.'

'You mean you thought it was unmanly to display your feelings, even at a time like that? So you just decided it was convenient to let little Christopher think so, too?'

As she expected, he faced her again on a tide of enraged defiance. 'What the hell do you know about it? Just because you've readl all the right books, think you're God's gift to all freaks and nutcases, do you think you can set yourself up as a judge? I tell you, lady, you won't climb inside this head however hard you try! Chris may be subject to a court order and I can't stop him coming here this time; but there's no way I have to sit here and be insulted.'

Anna sat back, surprised at the vehemence of his fury even though she had more or less engineered it. 'Mr Tyrell, your anger is not really directed at me. You're suffering from repressed emotion almost as much as your brother. What happened just then is known as transference: I made you pour out a bit of that inner feeling on to me. I'm not here to do that for you, but it's exactly what I hope to do for your brother. Now, once and for all, for his sake, will you co-operate?'

His strong features worked as he stared at her, dark with shock and resentment. She held her breath, wondering which way off the knife edge he would fall. She seemed coolly in charge, but there was actually no way of knowing how such a risk would turn out. She watched him dispassionately, a powerful male personality caught in a cleft stick by an equally positive female one.

It took several seconds, and then he subsided. For reasons of his own, he recovered his former wry scepticism in the face of her tactics. 'This is your professional judgment then, Dr Coleman?'

'For the moment, yes.'

'And if he's allowed to spit it all out, he'll be miraculously restored to his old cheery self?'

She smiled, leaning back in her chair and tapping the end of a pencil lightly on the desk. 'I don't promise anything. I only tell you the way I see the case. Until you let me know a lot more, Mr Tyrell, I can't pretend to understand, or begin to implement my theories properly.'

He cringed. '*Implement your theories . . . transference . . . repressed emotion.* You trick-cyclists have a language of your own, don't you? It all sounds like so much jargon to me, but then I'm just the ordinary guy in the street, aren't I? I can't be expected to penetrate your infinite wisdom?'

Anna smiled again, unruffled by his sneering. This was not real anger, as she had just witnessed it, but a much more superficial irritation, a pose. 'I have my suspicions,' she countered, 'that you're perfectly familiar with every phrase I've used. It just suits you, the role of the ignorant observer, doesn't it?'

'I'm not a fool,' he agreed, folding his arms and stretching out his long legs in front of him as he unwound, but still eyeing her warily. 'But I can't boast the high level of education that seems normal around here, I haven't got a string of letters after my name. Whatever I've achieved, I've done it without the benefit of university degrees.'

This confirmed Anna's earlier impression of the chip on his shoulder: a kind of inverted pride. 'What are your films about?' she enquired more gently. This was time to consolidate his support, not probe any deeper.

'Anything that grabs my fancy, providing the TV company forks out generous financial incentives. Tribal villages in the South American jungle, a kibbutz in Israel . . .'

'And so they always have to be in these far-flung places?'

'Not at all,' he retorted curtly. 'I've done plenty here: medical research, conservation issues, consumer exposés . . .'

'I suppose I should apologise for not having heard of you.' Anna's smile radiated her face with sudden charm, quite unexpected after their intense conversation.

Neil's gaze was arrested by it for several seconds; then he shrugged carelessly. 'I don't expect you'd remember if you had. We backroom boys only get a brief credit at the end, when all the viewers are switching off to go and make the cocoa, or busy discussing the programme among themselves.' He stated it as a fact, without rancour. If Anna had not heard differently, she might have believed him. She watched him, covertly but curiously, as he recaptured his ironic self-control. On familiar ground, dealing with his own subject, Neil Tyrell was composed, articulate, transparently clever despite his own protestations of lack of education.

He was less threatening too, she had to admit, when he was on surer territory. Up to then, his own insecurity in the face of this strange situation had turned itself far too easily into attacks on Anna's sensitive points. They were supposed to be well-protected, but he seemed to have an uncanny and alarming knack at exposing them.

He was leaning forward now, apparently deciding to pick up an earlier thread. 'If Chris was upset when I went away for long periods, he never showed it,' he asserted. 'And I want to assure you that he's never been left on his own. We have a highly efficient and trustworthy housekeeper who's been with us for years. She looks after him quite adequately when I'm away.'

'I'm sure she does,' Anna soothed. 'But as I've said before, a child needs more than that. He needs a warm supportive, expressive relationship with someone who really cares for him.'

'I care for him,' Neil stated tersely. 'His grandparents care for him. He used to go and stay with them several times a year till they got too old to cope. Mrs R cares for him—she always has.'

Anna frowned. 'Mrs R?'

'Our housekeeper: Mrs Robertson. We've always called her that; don't know why.'

'Ah—the efficient, trustworthy lady.'

'Precisely.'

But did the organising Mrs R offer tenderness? When Christopher was a small boy, had she been there with the loving affection he naturally needed? Anna had her doubts, but perhaps this was not the moment to follow them up. Plenty of time for that later, when sessions got under way. 'I'll take your word for it—for now.' She glanced at her watch, and the gesture did not go unnoticed.

'Is my allocated slot running out?' His smile was sardonic. 'Pity, I was just beginning to enjoy myself. You're much nicer, Dr Coleman, when you're not bullying some pathetic victim.'

'There's nothing the least pathetic about you, Mr Tyrell, and you're not a victim. You're not even my client. You're simply a client's family, which . . .'

'Which brings us back to good old Chris,' he interrupted rudely. 'So, what more can I say? You tell me I've got to help if I can. So okay, I'll help if I can. I'm prepared to admit, not that it would make the blindest bit of difference if I wasn't, that I made a serious mistake a year ago. I miscalculated, taking Chris away from you. I thought I was rescuing him from the clutches of an outfit that would just drive him deeper into the doldrums than ever. I thought I was doing the right thing; I can see now I wasn't.' Anna's gaze was steady on his as he made this confession. She knew it was costing him more than his attitude might suggest. 'Chris went from bad to worse,' he went on, suddenly bitter. 'Now he's drifted in with this undesirable lot who've started him off doing damn stupid things—the crazy little idiot, after all I've told him . . .' Neil turned away, his profile hard against the light from the window.

Anna was genuinely sympathetic. 'He never took his school leaving exams?'

'Not one. He's really bright but he never so much as wrote his name on a paper. Silly little bloody fool . . .' His hands clenched as anger and despair surged again from the depths where, Anna guessed, they always festered.

For the first time she stood up, and came round the desk to stand before him so that nothing separated them artificially. 'Don't get upset. You won't help Chris by going through it all again now. I promise you I'll do everything I can for him. With your help, I'm sure we can make it work, in the end.'

He looked her up and down as she leaned back on her desk, his fair brows arching. 'So what do we do first?' he demanded.

'I think I mentioned Family Therapy last year?' she ventured, remembering his reaction only too clearly.

'I think you did.' His mouth pursed up grimly but he made no comment.

'Well, all it means is that you both come in together on a regular basis, and we talk things through as a group, the three of us. Would you be prepared to do it?'

Neil was distinctly unwilling, but less openly hostile at least. 'Every time?'

'No; I'd want to see Christopher alone sometimes. Perhaps with you once a week, or once a fortnight if that's difficult.'

'And the idea is we get him to talk about the feelings he's never let out?' He was hesitant, deeply reluctant to commit himself.

'That's it. Sometimes things come out which only other members of a family can know.' Anna was calm, reassuring, but secretly willing him to agree.

'Hmmm.' He stared away into the middle distance; then his blue eyes focused on her again. 'Okay, I'll do it.' He grinned, and it was surprisingly boyish, almost disarming her. 'For you I'll do it.'

'Not for Christopher?' She frowned defensively, in mock disapproval.

'Who cares why I'm doing it? Maybe I just fancy being shut in here with a stunning lady psychologist for a few hours.' He rose to his feet in one swift movement so that he loomed unexpectedly close. He was back to where he had come in, deliberately teasing at the exposed corners of her carefully constructed shell. She stared boldly up into his eyes, now half a head above hers and regarding her with acute, wry perception. She felt overwhelmed, even menaced, and steeled herself: she had not gone through all this merely to lose the upper hand at the end.

'This is likely to be our only session entirely on our own,' she remarked sharply.

'You mean poor Chris has to take on the burden of chaperon, as if he didn't have enough to contend with?' Neil sighed satirically. 'My God, you experts know how to lay it on heavy.' Then he grinned and ran his fingers through the thickness of his fair hair. Responding involuntarily to the gesture as she watched, Anna decided the man was easier to cope with when he was angry than when he was amicable. 'So, when do we fix up the first of these little encounter groups?'

'This is in no way an encounter group,' she assured him firmly. 'Just three people having an informal chat.'

'Or two having a chat and a third putting in an odd unhelpful snort if we're lucky,' he amended caustically.

'We'll see.' Anna walked sedately out of his force field—which simply stretched out after her—towards the secure haven behind her desk. 'You might be amazed.'

'I might at that, Dr Coleman.' He watched her lazily as she flicked through the pages of her diary, deliberately avoiding his eyes.

'I'm seeing Christopher on Monday, then Thursday. Could you come on Thursday?'

'Then once a week, or what?' He was suspicious again now, the mask back in place.

'Shall we take it slowly—say once a fortnight for the time being?'

'I should be able to manage that. I'm not taking on any new assignments until this business is sorted out once and for all.'

Anna glanced at him, noting the clouding of his eyes, the steely resolution in his voice. 'That's good.' With the solidity of her desk between them once more, she risked a breezy smile. 'Thanks for coming, Mr Tyrell. I'll see you next week.'

'Thursday it is. I'll equip myself with a box of man-sized tissues.' On this sardonically cryptic note he left her, pulling the door shut behind him.

Just as she had done a year ago, Anna found herself staring after him, pen poised over her notes. Their interaction was the same—or was it? She could hardly describe the interview just concluded as an action replay of that other, earlier one. Something had changed, moved, clicked during those months; but was it in him, or her? Or even in both of them? Or was she getting fanciful, imagining things? If so, she must take a grip on herself; that would never do. Clients and their families must be kept in their rightful place: voices in a room, words in a file . . .

Squaring her shoulders, she dragged her attention back to formulating a brisk, official version of the complex exchanges she had just had with Neil Tyrell.

For some reason, it was far harder than usual to shape her very personal responses into concise technical phrases in her neatly flowing hand.

CHAPTER THREE

ANNA lived contentedly alone in a small flat which comprised the top floor of a tall Edwardian terraced house in one of the most ordinary roads in Islington. Until six months ago she had shared a house with a motley collection of people in West Hampstead, but she had never really felt cut out for the communal life. After a couple of years she had grown tired of the constant need to refer every minor change or decision to the group, yearning for real independence, a place of her own. She was too busy and preoccupied with work to contemplate buying one, with all the hassle involved, so she simply studied the *To Let* advertisements in magazines and evening papers till she found what she wanted.

It was handy for the clinic, reasonably cheap, and totally bare so that Anna could imprint her own personality on it. Gradually, over the weeks, she had picked up furniture and other necessities, poking about in markets and obscure shops at weekends until she found just the right bits and pieces. Now the flat was basically equipped, but it lacked those extra touches—luxuries, idiosyncrasies—which really make a home. Somehow Anna had got stuck at this stage and never seemed to get round to adding them. Her attitude to life was simple and functional, leaving little room for indulgences.

Her upbringing had pointed her firmly in this direction. She came from a joining of two stocks which both considered hard work the be-all and end-all of existence, placing strict limitations on useless enjoyment. Born in a Yorkshire city, the only child of parents already well into their thirties and set in a rigid framework of living, Anna had been planned and welcomed, but without much demonstrative enthusiasm.

47

The little girl soon learned to keep her emotional needs under control, applying her outstanding energy and intelligence to mastering as many skills as possible because this pleased her parents more than anything. All through school, academic achievement was the one thing which brought smiles and loving approval from them; so Anna concentrated on that, with brilliant results.

She was (as her education had now taught her) a classic product of hybrid vigour: the mingling of two distinct genetic strains, creating a unique freshness and originality. Her parents had married against the wishes of both their families. Her father's people were solid English tradesmen, owners of a local grocery business which had been extended over several generations into a thriving chain of small shops. Her father's older brother had been keen to take on the firm, leaving Frank Coleman to follow his own instincts, which had taken the form of staying on at school (a fairly rare decision in that family), getting himself well and truly educated and then training to be an optician. A few years later he was proudly running his own successful business in the centre of the city.

During these years, the young Frank's chief leisure activity (in fact more or less his only leisure activity) was singing in a choral society which met once a week in a draughty church hall. While they rehearsed for an amateur performance of Bach's *St Matthew Passion*, he had noticed a fellow-member, a young woman with black hair and brown eyes and a shy, radiant smile. Her name was Rose Solomons. Frank, immediately captivated, spent his Tuesday evenings staring at her as discreetly as possible over the top of his score as they faced each other across the choir stalls, he among the tenors and she among the altos. As far as he could tell, Rose had not noticed his attentions; but in fact she chose the rare moments when he looked down at his music to glance up and study him covertly, no less fascinated or attracted than he was.

Eventually he had plucked up the courage to talk to

her, and their friendship had quickly blossomed and ripened into love. Within a few months Frank had proposed and Rose had accepted. This should have been the beginning of their mutual happiness, but it was where their troubles started. Rose's family were Jewish immigrants from central Europe. Her father, a doctor, had been brought to England as a child; her mother, a professional musician, had been born in Yorkshire but to recently settled parents. Both had been raised in a strong tradition of keeping to their own kind, their own way of life. When Frank and Rose announced their engagement, it created a stir which spread ripples far and wide among two quite separate communities. There was equal opposition on both sides, but the young couple were determined and spirited and very much in love, so they cut themselves off from family disapproval and went their own way.

Rose was studying to be a dentist and she simply continued her chosen profession, pausing only after a good few years, when she was already a partner in a busy practice, to have Anna and then dutifully take care of her until she started at a nursery school. From the time Anna was three, her mother had always worked, and the child grew used to the fact that both her parents were absorbed in their careers as well as in each other, leaving her place in their life probably a poor third. She accepted her situation, even counted her blessings. At least she never lacked for anything: she had security, and she knew at heart that she had their love. She grew up as beautiful, accomplished and self-contained as her mother; and she inherited her mother's deeply implanted belief in women's need for, and right to, a life of their own—not to be dictated to by the demands of men and children. Many of Rose's female relatives had been successful in worldly terms, though not without a struggle in some cases, whether it was in the professions or the arts or the even more male-dominated fields of science and technology. One aunt had even been a renowned anthropological explorer.

These somewhat radical opinions alienated Frank's

more conventional parents still further, and over the
years neither family ever really accepted the liaison,
even though it soon became obvious that the couple
were making a success of their life together. Anna was
doted on by both sets of grandparents, who lavished all
the care and affection on her which was missing at
home. Afterwards, she reflected they had probably
saved her sanity. But by the time she was twenty and at
university locally, all four of them had died, and she
still missed them terribly, even now.

On graduating, she had escaped to London to take
her higher degree and work towards her diploma. Anna
had always been intrigued by the way minds work –
what makes people tick – and psychology was the only
subject she ever really wanted to study. She had never
regretted it; and perhaps it was her own early
experiences that had pushed her into the specialist
branch dealing with children. Anyway, one thing was
certain: her reaction to cases like Christopher Tyrell's
(which were depressingly common) went deeper than
mere academic interest. They touched a raw, exposed
nerve, even through all the layers of training and self-
discipline.

Anna's parents were both still alive and well and
living in the same semi in the residential suburb where
she had grown up. She corresponded with them quite
regularly, with more duty than pleasure, but she rarely
went to see them; and they had visited her only twice in
the whole time she'd been in London. They trusted her
to take care of herself and took it for granted that any
daughter of theirs would shine at her chosen career and
keep her private life under control. Rose had a sister
living in Golders Green with her family, and Anna saw
them a few times a year; but on the whole she neither
needed nor expected contact with any of them.

Arriving home this Thursday evening, she heaved a
sigh of relief as she locked up her car and rummaged in
her bag for her house keys. It had been a trying day. It
would be wonderful to put her feet up, perhaps listen to
some Mozart on her stereo (one of the few luxuries she

allowed herself), have a cup of tea and a piece of that ginger cake she'd baked last weekend. It should be just about moist enough by now in its tin, ready to eat . . .

Anna cherished a secret, almost illicit passion for cooking—especially baking—often spending her week-ends in the kitchen, happily producing pies and puddings, cakes and quiches which fed her through the ensuing frenetic week. She felt oddly uncomfortable about this, and preferred not to let too many people know about it, assuring herself it was an ideal therapy after hours of intense brainwork, smiling ruefully at her own sense of guilt as she stirred some delicious concoction or other.

It suited Anna, being alone. Throughout her days at college and after, she had made plenty of friends, but no close ones. She kept them at a careful distance, always following up advances just so far and no further. She was popular but private, rarely showing her true self to anyone. When work was over she liked to retire into her own space and keep the world at bay. As for the men who frequently saw fit to try and penetrate her armour of innocence, she gave them short shrift, having neither time nor inclination for anything of that kind. She had successfully suppressed her natural urges in that direction, along with everything else that failed to fit in with her circumspect view of life, and was proud of it.

Of course she knew all about the sexual drive, the connections between emotional and mental states and behavioural patterns. Her dark head brimmed with theories, a wide and profound knowledge of everything that contributes to the human psyche. On paper it was impressive, and it made her an expert at her job. But, as Daniel had rightly realised, her self-discipline was also a severe limitation. Anna lacked that essential spark, that quality of being a part of humanity, a member of a species with shared emotions and experiences. Her senior colleague admired her single-mindedness, but he regretted it too, for the clients' sake as well as her own.

Now she walked slowly up the stairs, past the ground

floor flat where the elderly landlady lived with her three
cats, two budgies and a lifetime's collection of bric-à-
brac. Past the door to the middle flat, occupied by her
ideal neighbour, Jonathan Dawes, who had quickly
proved a comforting, supportive new friend on her
doorstep. He made few demands, and she liked him a
lot—though she suspected he'd willingly have pushed
their relationship into something closer if she had given
him the slightest encouragement. She didn't, of course,
and it saddened her that men seemed to find it so hard
to accept her friendship on a platonic level.

Jonathan was a musician, a jobbing composer, clever
and eager but still eluded by real success. He'd had some
songs published, and arranged existing works for use in
radio and television series. One of his popular numbers
had hit a high spot in the charts, and he was still living
on the strength of it, both financially and spiritually.
Climbing up the last flight of stairs, Anna heard the
strains of his beloved piano echoing through his door.
He would sit there for hours, working out his themes
and harmonies, or just playing for his own pleasure,
boogying and vamping away at the old blues and
ballads that were his real favourites.

This was what he was doing now. Anna smiled as the
familiar soulful words and melody reached her:

> 'They asked me how I knew
> My true love was true,
> I, of course, replied,
> Something here inside
> Cannot be denied . . .'

She let herself quietly into her flat, dumped her bags
and washed her hands; then she set about the soothing
ritual of making tea.

'Damn!' Opening the fridge to get out the milk, she
remembered she had run out of it that morning. She'd
intended to buy some on the way home, but the events
of the day had driven it clean from her mind.

She checked in her cupboard, but without much
hope, for the tin of skimmed milk powder: no, just as

she thought, she'd used the last of it on Sunday in a batter. She must remember to add it to her shopping list. She hated her tea black, so there was only one thing for it. Leaving her door on the latch, she ran downstairs and knocked on Jonathan's.

> *'Now, laughing friends deride*
> *Tears I cannot hide,*
> *So I smile and say,*
> *When a lovely flame dies*
> *Smoke gets in your eyes . . .'*

The music tailed off and there was the sound of the stool scraping back as Jonathan detached himself reluctantly from the piano and came to answer the summons. But when he saw Anna, his thin, rather mournful face lit up. 'Anna! Back already? Is that really the time?' He pushed back a threadbare sleeve to look at his watch. 'So it is. How was your day?'

'Not too bad thanks, Jon,' she said automatically. 'I'm on the scrounge, I'm afraid. Can you spare a bit of milk? I'm making tea, and I've . . .'

'Sure, of course.' He turned to lead her through to his small kitchen, the same compact shape as her own but strikingly less clean and organised. 'Better still,' he invited, swinging round to face her in the tiny hallway, 'why don't I make you some tea down here? I haven't spoken to a living soul all day. I could use a bit of intelligent company.'

'I suppose I qualify as a living soul,' Anna said with a wry grin, 'but I'm not so sure about the intelligent company. If you want to know the truth, I've had one hell of a day.'

Jonathan peered closely into her face through his metal-framed spectacles. 'You do look a bit strained, Anna. All the more reason,' he stated firmly, 'to let me look after you. Come on, no argument. Go up and shut your door—switch off your kettle if it's on—and let Uncle Jon minister to you for once.'

'For once? You're always ministering to me! Anyway, I interrupted you . . .'

'Good grief, I was only doodling. The muse is not upon me today. I've sat there for about five hours, and scribbled all of three lines. I think I'm suffering from Composer's Block.' His pleasant, humorous features drooped satirically. 'If you don't rescue me from myself, I'll go up the wall. I need you to bring me a breath of fresh air from the big wide world,' he wheedled.

Anna laughed and gave in. It was a tempting prospect, if she was honest, a relaxing chat with Jonathan over a cup of tea in his cosy chaotic sitting room, where it was quite a pioneering enterprise to find a seat among the stacks of scores, sheet music and manuscript paper. 'Okay, thanks. I'll just pop up, then.'

Back in her flat, she grabbed her key and the tin containing the ginger cake, released the latch on her door and clicked it behind her. Within ten minutes she was sitting opposite Jonathan as he poured tea from a pot shaped like a ridiculous head with a grinning face, a hat for a lid, a nose for a spout, and a pair of surreal feet sticking out underneath. Cutting two generous chunks of the cake, Anna put them on to plates and pushed one across the cluttered coffee table towards him.

'Mmmm!' he murmured, gazing at it appreciatively. 'Lovely and sticky—just right. And you say I'm the one who ministers to *you*?'

'Well, perhaps it's fairly equal after all,' she conceded. 'What we in the trade call a collusion.'

'As long as you continue to supply me with home-baked offerings,' Jonathan declared, 'I'm only too happy to keep up my side of the collusion any time you like. You know I'm always pleased to see you, Anna.' His light tone became briefly serious. 'You don't have to wait till you run out of milk.'

'No, well—I'm not at my best after a tough day,' she hedged.

'What was extra tough about this one?' Jonathan enquired. 'Wow!' He munched his piece of cake while Anna deliberated whether to tell him or not. 'This is the best yet! How do you get this texture, all soft and gooey? When I tried to make it once, it turned out like a slab of well-tanned leather.'

Anna smiled, biting into her own slice. 'You've got to make sure the eggs are well beaten, and use syrup as well as molasses or black treacle. It's sinful, really.'

'What's a bit of sinful stodge between consenting adults?' Jonathan chanted airily, but his light blue eyes were sharp on her face. 'So, are you going to tell me about this tough day of yours, or not?'

Anna sighed. 'Well, you remember I had this case which reappeared out of the blue after being shelved a year ago? I think I told you about it on Monday.'

'You bet I remember—the boy and his ferocious brother: fascinating stuff. Was today the next instalment, then?' He demolished his cake, still watching her.

'It was,' confirmed Anna tautly.

'Not so good?' he prompted sympathetically.

'You could say that.' Anna sipped her tea, relishing its aromatic steam. 'The boy's really gone under. I can't seem to get through to him at all. And on top of that, today I was suddenly presented with his brother again—just like that. No time to prepare, or anything. An hour's private session.' Her gaze darkened and wandered away to a corner of the room; a faint flush stained her cheeks.

Jonathan's attention was immediately caught by her expression. He had never seen it before: deeply unsettled, almost haunted. 'So tell me what happened? This brother hasn't mellowed, I gather, with the passing of time?'

'Far from it.' Anna's soft mouth twisted grimly. 'Quite the reverse. The boy's problems are serious now, and I can see why. At least, I'm beginning to see why, but there are aspects of the story I need to get to the bottom of. I've got a feeling I'm only just starting. It's not going to be easy.'

'Is this older brother still being obstructive, then?'

Anna considered, as if for her own benefit, how best to answer Jonathan's question. 'Not exactly ob-

structive—not in the way he was a year ago.' She
thought about it, weighing up the words slowly as she
said them. 'He can't stop Christopher coming to us now
anyway, because there's a drugs sentence pending and
the court's ordered him to attend the Unit. No, but
there's something about him—I can't quite put my
finger on it—he's unreasonably reluctant to join in,
even to help Christopher; and I'm absolutely sure he
genuinely wants to help him. I suppose he's just afraid
of being probed, exposed, like most people are . . .' she
mused, half to herself. Then she lifted her chin
triumphantly and looked directly across at Jonathan.
'But I persuaded him in the end,' she declared. 'He's
agreed to come to some sessions, for Christopher's
sake. Starting next week.'

'Well done, Anna!' Jonathan's praise was sincere. He
knew just how much Anna's work meant to her, and
regarded her dedication with a kind of tolerant awe.
'What sort of bloke is this older brother?' he persisted,
sensing that Anna needed to talk about it—and also
acutely curious himself about the rare man who could
arouse such strong responses in her, even if they were
basically hostile.

'Oh . . .' She shrugged carelessly, then chewed her
cake and drank her tea, playing for time. 'Rather big
and powerful—you know the type—I've never liked
them much. Oozing confidence, emanating success.
Clever, but understated; hides behind irony all the time.
Defensive, when it comes to personal matters.' She
paused for a few moments, and then admitted with a
touch of unwilling fascination, 'I suppose he could be
very charming—in the right context.'

Jonathan's interest deepened. 'Success at what? What
line is he in?'

'He describes himself as a media-man. Makes films
for television, as I understand it. I don't know what he
officially calls himself: producer, director or what. It's
all mysterious to me, television, as you know. All I
know is, the job takes him away half the time, which
has not helped poor Christopher one bit.'

'What did you say his name was?' Jonathan, a TV addict, was leaning forward now, eyes fixed eagerly on her face.

'I didn't. And you know very well I shouldn't, Jonathan. It's all confidential.'

'Oh go on, Anna! you know it'll be safe with me. I'm the soul of discretion. And,' he switched on his mildest, most reasonable tone—which did nothing to conceal the burning curiosity beneath, 'you never know, I might be able to offer some useful background information on the guy, if I've heard of him.'

Anna knew she could trust Jonathan, but over the years she had trained herself to be immune to such coaxings. It was more than her reputation was worth to let her natural interest in a client overcome that vital discretion essential in all caring and healing professions. 'Sorry, Jon.' She grinned to soften the blow. 'No can do; you should know that by now. Maybe one day, when the case is all sewn up . . .'

He nodded ruefully, holding up one hand to stop her going on. 'Okay, okay, Doc Coleman. Point taken. Keep my big nose out of the details.' He drained his tea, then his face brightened. 'But that doesn't mean you can't regale me with the general gist of their problems. Even if they're just Mr X and his unfortunate younger brother Christopher. You know I'm always here and willing, Anna,' he added more seriously, 'if you ever feel a need to talk a case through with someone objective— on a strictly anonymous basis, of course.'

She smiled again. 'I know that, Jonathan, and I'm grateful.'

Jonathan waited to see if she would take him up on his hopeful offer, but when she simply sipped her tea, he pressed on. 'I suppose dynamic, creative people are often the most mixed-up?' he suggested.

'It's not quite as straightforward as that.' Deliberately, delicately, Anna let herself pick up his thread. 'This man's not what I'd call mixed-up; not in the way his brother is. But they both suffered severe trauma when they lost their parents.'

'You mean they died?'

'There was some kind of accident and they were both killed, that's all I know—as yet. The case notes are strangely thin on that point, and I have to tread very carefully when it comes to rooting out the details. I can't risk frightening either of them off. I've got to choose my moment and my tactics with extreme precision.'

Jonathan glanced quizzically at the determined set of her chin, the gleam in her eye; then he spread his loose-limbed frame more comfortably on his shabby sofa. 'I'm inclined to pity this guy,' he mused. 'I bet he doesn't realise the grilling he's in for. Gale warnings should be hoisted on all fronts.'

Anna returned his wicked grin. 'As you've never been at the receiving end of my technique, Jon, I can only assure you I'm known for my tactful and subtle approach. I'm not in the business of hurting people, unless I absolutely have to.'

And what about you? Jonathan's expression clearly wondered. *Are you so strong, so proof against being hurt, Anna?* But he held his peace, quietly listening as she went vehemently on, 'The boy might well have to suffer before he can be released from his depression. As for the man,' her eyes flashed defiance, 'he's tough enough to take whatever we throw at him. Don't waste any pity on him.'

Jonathan hunched his shoulders. 'On second thoughts, perhaps envy might be nearer the mark,' he observed laconically. 'If I have to manufacture a nervous breakdown before I get to be at the receiving end of your technique, I'll start working on it straight away.' He was joking, of course—but only just.

'Jonathan!' Anna's glare was reproachful. 'It's not something to be funny about. The anguish involved can be appalling. If you could only see . . .' Then she caught his ironically apologetic, hangdog expression—and they both burst out laughing together.

CHAPTER FOUR

MONDAY'S session with Christopher was not encouraging. This time he slumped listlessly, head bowed,
exuding melancholy from beneath a veneer of studied
boredom. From time to time a large clumsy foot would
kick out against the edge of the low table which stood
between their chairs, as if he was suddenly overwhelmed
with a hopeless aggression, but then he would subside
again into silent gloom. Try as she might, Anna could
get nothing out of him except the occasional long hard
stare when he evidently considered one of her questions
or comments particularly facile. Most of the time he
avoided her eyes and kept his reactions, if he had any,
to himself.

'Christopher,' she appealed to him urgently, just
before the hour was up. 'You do know I'm trying to
help you, don't you?'

He looked up at her, and she read in his blue eyes a
turmoil of bewildered doubt. Then, just as she was
about to give up for the day and dismiss him, he
nodded. A slight, almost imperceptible movement of
the head, but undoubtedly a nod. Her heart leaping,
Anna fought to prevent her face breaking out into a
beam. Instead she nodded gravely in return as she stood
up, collecting her papers together. 'That's good,
because I most certainly am,' she said quietly.

For the next two days, as she dealt efficiently with
her other clients, Anna's mind kept returning to that
magic moment. The first response from a deeply
depressed patient was always the most exciting part of
her work. Trepidation about what would happen when
Neil joined them on Thursday tinged her pleasure in
this tiny achievement.

She needn't have worried. As soon as Neil and
Christopher arrived, it was obvious the boy was more

relaxed, perhaps even pleased to have his brother's positive participation. Neil, on the other hand, was guarded, tight-lipped with inner tension. Nothing would induce him to let Christopher down, but it was clear he was there on sufferance and fully expected to dislike every minute of it.

Anna, at her most unruffled, greeted them with polite serenity. She never cut herself off behind her desk during actual sessions, believing it to be important to create an atmosphere of informal equality. The three of them sat in comfortable upholstered armchairs around the small wooden table. The case file lay closed in Anna's lap while she adroitly manipulated the mood of their conversation into the directions she wanted it to take.

'First off,' she smiled at Christopher, 'I'd like to hear any stories Neil can tell us about when you were very young. For a start, let's see how he remembers the day you were born, shall we?'

Anns had her carefully considered reasons for this opening gambit, and they were proved justified when Christopher repeated the same slight nod, but with increased emphasis. Anna turned calmly to Neil, whose expression of veiled reluctance had given way to surprise at her proposal, and then astonishment at Christopher's reaction. 'Can you remember, Neil? Where were you at the time?' she prompted.

'The day Chris was born?' He sat back, crossing long legs clad in cream canvas, levelling a quizzical blue gaze on to her. 'Well, Dr Coleman . . .' His tone was ironic as usual—but only faintly, so as not to upset his brother.

'Anna,' she cut in at once. 'Now that we're all here, please call me Anna. You too, Christopher, of course,' she added seriously, as if there was much hope of him calling her anything. Then she turned enquiring hazel eyes back to Neil. 'Sorry, I interrupted you?'

'Well, Anna . . .' He studied her, folding his arms. It seemed to her he deliberately stressed her name, relishing it on his tongue, staring at her as if to decide whether it suited her or not. She had instructed him to use it, as she always did to every new client—and yet the sound of it on his lips caused her to tingle, even to tremble, in a way no self-respecting professional counsellor had any right to do. He smiled slightly, as if reading her reaction clearly, but then he turned to his brother and continued in a calm, steady tone. 'As it happens, I remember it very well. Chris came on the scene in January—right, Chris?' He smiled at the boy, who actually nodded again. The change Neil's presence had already created in him was astounding. If only she could concentrate on that, rather than the effect he was having on her!

'It was about three weeks after Christmas.' Neil was relaxing a little himself now. 'The parents had been to Switzerland at New Year. Everyone went on at Mother for going away so near the time she was due.' Anna cast Christopher a quick glance to see how he was taking this cool mention of their parents. He showed no sign of being upset, simply following Neil's every syllable with rapt attention. Relieved, since she didn't want to delve too deeply at this early stage, Anna turned back to Neil.

'The doctor said she could go if she promised not even to attempt to ski; the air would do her good.' Neil grinned reminiscently. 'Mother said she only ever went for the *après-ski* anyway and she was quite content to cheer Father's prowess on the slopes from the sidelines—but she wasn't missing her last unencumbered holiday for anyone, baby or no baby. So she went.' His tone and expression were becoming less strained as memory took over. 'Mother was like that—wasn't she?' he appealed to Christopher, as if it was the most natural thing to do.

Anna held her breath, but it was all right: Christopher merely nodded again, still not taking his eyes from his brother's face. Anna had the sensation of witnessing a machine, severely stuck and seized up, responding to a dose of oil and grinding at last into creaky action.

'She was a strong character, was Mother.' Neil was doing a grand job, for someone so unwilling to be doing it at all. Anna had to marvel at his own strength of character; obviously it was hereditary. Respect for this unpredictable man was sneaking up on her. 'Father adored her, so we knew he'd look after her okay. They had a great time. Everyone made a fuss of her. I've rarely seen her look better than when they got home. Mother was one of those women who really thrive on being pregnant.' He gazed reflectively at Christopher as if seeing him in a new light. 'She looked radiant the whole time she was carrying you, Chris. Glowing.'

It was a flat statement of fact but it reached a target, whether intentionally or not. A faint but distinct answering glow appeared on the boy's waxy cheeks. Neil had paused, and Anna shot him a supportive glance. Meeting it, he smiled at her: the most straightforward smile she'd seen from him yet. Then he turned back to Christopher and went on. 'You were born just two weeks later, on exactly the day you were due. They all said how convenient it was, and what a good baby you were—and how like me you looked. I didn't take that as a compliment,' he added drily. 'You looked more like an over-stewed prune to me.'

Anna wondered how Christopher would respond to this affectionate teasing. The coins of red deepened in his cheeks and he bowed his head. Several tantalising seconds later, he lifted it again—and he was smiling. A small, sheepish smirk, hovering at one corner of his mouth and soon vanishing, but definitely there.

They both saw it, and exchanged quick glances of satisfaction. Then Anna asked Neil, determined to keep things moving, 'I don't suppose you'd had much to do with small babies up to then?'

'Nothing whatever,' he confirmed with a wry grin. 'But I soon learned. They weren't leaving *me* out of this new bit of excitement,' he stated meaningfully. 'I appointed myself babysitter-in-chief. Pretty soon, what I didn't know about nappies and bottles and bringing up burps wasn't worth knowing.'

'Well,' Anna declared, leaning back in her chair, 'that's one hundred per cent more than *I* know about it, I'll tell you that for nothing!'

Christopher was smiling again, even more convincingly this time. Breakthrough, Anna thought euphorically—this is it, the moment of breakthrough—the machine gathering impetus! *But don't count your chickens*, her sensible mind warned; *many a slip* . . . as if she didn't know that by now, only too well. Containing her pleasure, she turned back to Neil and went on, 'I thought you were at boarding school? How come you were at home when Chris was a baby?'

'I left after the fifth form,' he explained tersely. 'I refused to stay on after I was sixteen—and anyway, when I heard about Mother's Interesting Condition, I made up my mind not to be excluded. I came home and did my A-levels at the local Tech; and a great improvement it was, too.'

The rest of the hour followed the same pattern. Quietly determined, Neil continued to supply them with anecdotes about Christopher's infancy, creating a very real, warm sense of that early family life. While she provided firm but unobtrusive guidance, Anna watched and listened closely for signs of repressed jealousy in Neil himself; but if there were any, or ever had been, he successfully hid them. Either he had become a past-master at controlling them over the years, or he was even cannier than he seemed, beating Anna at her own game.

From what she was now learning about the man, the latter was more than possible. She wouldn't put it past Neil Tyrell to be as aware of her tactics as she was herself. But she must hold on to the reins; it was more vital than ever to stay in charge now that things really did look more promising.

Between them they took Christopher carefully through the first few years of his life, digging out memories ranging from major to trivial, through never too alarming. The boy remained engrossed and alert, but still he never uttered a single word. When at last

Anna declared it was time to stop, Christopher rose unexpectedly to his feet—a gangling figure, towering temporarily over them—and, even more disconcertingly, found his tongue.

'Got to have a pee,' he muttered without ceremony; then he slouched to the door, opened it and disappeared along the corridor.

Left alone, Anna and Neil stared at one another, equally taken aback by this down-to-earth conclusion to an intense hour. Then, spontaneously and simultaneously, they dissolved into relieved laughter.

'Well, Dr Cole ... Anna.' Languid after the emotional tension and exertion, Neil yawned, stretching long arms above his fair head. 'How did you think that little lot went? Did I satisfy requirements?'

'It went better than I could have hoped, Neil. I can't tell you how pleased I am. You were ...' she swallowed the praise she was tempted to shower upon him, reminding herself of the necessity to keep things businesslike. 'You really tried, and I know it wasn't easy. I do believe we'll get somewhere, if we go on like that.'

'A bit like hard work, isn't it?' Neil stood up and walked to the window, where he stared broodingly out, thrusting his hands deep into his pockets.

'And it'll probably get harder,' Anna commented darkly. 'Think you can take it?'

He swung round. 'If that's what Chris needs, I'll take as much of it as you like—within reason. So far,' he pointed out, 'we haven't exactly covered any sensitive ground, have we?'

'That's true. But some people might have found today's session hopelessly demanding,' Anna assured him. 'You've got the—the moral stamina to cope, I'd say.'

His eyes narrowed. 'That's a professional judgment, I take it, as opposed to a personal one?'

'Of course it's my professional opinion, but I can't draw a hard line between the two,' Anna countered with cool honesty.

Neil turned back to the window. 'How did Monday's session go?'

'Badly. You wouldn't have recognised Christopher as the same person. In fact, Neil, if you'd . . .' Still sitting in her chair, Anna leaned towards him, her face lit by eagerness. 'Would you consider coming to *all* the sessions for a while? I know I said only once a fortnight, but after today I've changed my mind. If we tackle this jointly, twice a week, keep up the momentum, I think we'll really be on to something.' She paused, waiting for his reaction, but he remained silent so she stepped up the persuasion. 'If I have to see him on his own three times in four, or even one time in two, I'm afraid we'll lose the progress we make when you're here, too.'

Neil managed to express sarcasm, even with his back. '*If* we continue to make progress, when I'm here, too,' he observed.

'If we do; of course no one's promising anything,' Anna agreed evenly. Then, when he still failed to reply, she pressed, 'Please, Neil? I could be really optimistic if you would. I'm sure Christopher's only beginning to respond the way he did because you're here. He appreciates having your . . .' she hesitated, fearful of straying on to thin ice just now, '. . . help,' she finished lamely.

'My undivided attention for once, is what you were about to say.' Neil's voice was hard, but when he turned back to Anna he was smiling thinly. 'I take your point, Anna. I'm well aware of your theories on that subject. Okay then, I'll come, if that's what's prescribed by the expert lady.'

'Thanks, Neil.' She smiled her grateful relief. 'I'm sure it'll be well worth your extra time. You won't regret it.'

He shrugged. 'I've told you, flower, I'm making this whole thing a top priority till Chris is back to his normal self, or something near it. I've having no more nonsense about dope, or glue, or any other damn fool escape from reality. If this is how I get my brother back, then this is what I'll do—even if it means coming here every day.'

'Good.' Anna got up and took her papers over to the desk. 'And when you're both at home, just act as ordinarily as possible. Chat to him if you see him but try not to discuss things we talk about here,' she advised.

'Chance would be a fine thing.' Neil left the window to come and stand near the desk. 'I never see him at home unless I ferret him out of his den. He lurks in that room all the time, especially since the court hearing. Except for these little outings, of course, when the combined influences of two pretty social workers and myself, not to mention Mrs R, are often required to manoeuvre him out of the house.'

'Perhaps that'll be different now,' she suggested gently. 'You never know.'

'Maybe.' He picked up his jacket from the back of a chair and walked to the door. 'I'd better go and see what the hell he's doing; he's been long enough.'

'I expect he's waiting for you in reception. It would be quite natural for him not to want to come back in here after a session like that,' Anna explained.

Neil paused at the door, jacket hooked over an index finger to hang down behind one shoulder. 'I'll take your word for it, Doctor.' Then he opened the door, flashed her one of those sudden disarming smiles, and was gone.

His abrupt departure left a peculiar emptiness, a strong sense of disappointment. 'See you Monday!' Anna called after him, into the vacuum, wondering at her own abnormal sensitivity. The more her confidence in the case built up, the more her vulnerability seemed to grow where the man was concerned. She sighed, listening to her words echoing into the deserted corridor. There was no reply.

That weekend, she found it necessary to tackle a particularly demanding batch of baking, keeping her thoughts and feelings well submerged under constructive activity. The Tyrell case, and the Tyrell man, had got under her skin in a way no case should and no man ever had. Exasperation with herself for allowing this to happen battled with excited anticipation. How would Neil rise to the challenge at the next week's session? How would it all work itself out?

Neil did not let her down. Apparently well in control of himself, though occasionally retiring behind that screen of irony for a few moments, he let her lead him slowly but surely through more recollections of Christopher's childhood. Anna knew it was costing him, exposing those memories for his brother's sake, and her respect for him increased with every minute. She suspected his efforts would pay off in the end, for his own benefit as well as Christopher's. She could only hope so.

Christopher absorbed it all, obviously revelling in it, his gaze never leaving Neil's face. Even when directly addressed he still refused to speak, but when Neil produced an amusing story he managed a weak grin, and sometimes Anna thought his expression might be about to crumple at last. But he wasn't ready yet to let out any deeper emotions. There was more ground to cover before that.

At the end of Thursday's hour, when Christopher had effected his usual swift exit, Anna stared meditatively after him. 'If he actually breaks down, we'll know things are really on the move,' she said quietly.

Neil stood by the window, tired and strained by the session, his face dark with effort. 'You mean he might bawl and scream? Scenes of emotional carnage?'

'I've never pretended he won't have to suffer in the process, if it's to work.' Anna leaned back against her desk, regarding him intently. Superficially she was composed, but underneath she was wondering rather frantically just how this face, this form in front of her could have filled up her mind as quickly and thoroughly as it had. By what ridiculous magic could anyone become so familiar, so welcome in her consulting room, after such a short time? Since when had . . .?

'No.' His voice was sharp, cutting into her rambling thoughts. 'You've never pretended, Anna.' He smiled grimly across at her. 'And you never pretended it would be any picnic for me, either. I've faced a few tricky situations in my time, some tough challenges, but nothing that drags as deep as this.'

'I know, Neil,' she said softly. 'And that's why it's wonderful of you to be doing this with such—such devotion.'

Abruptly, as if her words had touched a trigger, he pulled his hands from his pockets and came over to her: two fast strides were enough to bring him within inches. Anna, trapped by her own desk and frozen in a kind of stunned fascination, could only gaze into his face. She had never, in the whole of her life, felt so acutely aware of anyone or anything as this man—this warm powerful body now all but touching hers. It was a new awareness on a new scale: painful, exhilarating, swamping all reason. She drew in a shuddering, steadying breath.

'If anyone's being devoted, Anna, it's you.' Neil's voice was low but vibrant. He stood so close she could feel his breath fanning her skin. 'You know full well I'd never have taken this thing on in the first place if you hadn't convinced me it was the only way. Without your skill, these sessions could be a disaster area.'

His hands grasped her shoulders, sending shock waves coursing freely in all directions. Fortunately he was still speaking, because there was no way she could have found her voice just then. 'After all, Chris is my brother. Maybe it's partly my fault he's like he is.' Neil's expression tightened. 'I've got a potent incentive to see all this through. I'm involved, whether I like it or not; I can see that now, thanks to you. But you . . .'

He tailed off and his hands slid down her arms to rest just above her elbows, but his eyes continued their intense search of her face. Anna took advantage of the pause to crash in with her own unthinking defence reflex. His tone and touch were far too personal, far too intimate for her liking. Now she gathered all her resources into dispelling the mood he had created, pushing them both on to safer ground. 'Whereas I am just doing my job. The work I'm trained—and paid—to do.'

Neil reacted instantly to the blunt words, dropping his hands and stepping back, his eyes hardening. 'Of course, just doing your job. I was forgetting.' He turned away, running his fingers through his hair in a gesture which had become extraordinarily haunting to her. His broad frame, usually so upright, drooped wearily. Anna's heart called out to him but she stayed where she was, clutching the edge of the desk behind her. 'Well, let's hope I can keep up with the pace,' he muttered, shooting her a last wry glance as he made for the door.

At once Anna was flooded with remorse, mentally kicking herself for her pathetic rejection of his attempt to make real contact. She should be ashamed, a woman with her experience of psychological interaction ... trained in counselling ...

But that was just it, of course; it had been the woman, not the psychologist, who had risen to defend her threatened autonomy. There was a conflict there, too profound even for her understanding. Neil had stirred up a complex area which had lain dormant all her life, and she had no professional wisdom, no convenient textbooks, for dealing with it.

Dreading the long weekend ahead, especially if things were left like this, she took a faltering step towards him. 'Neil, I didn't ...'

But he cut her off short as he turned the door handle. 'Mustn't keep little brother waiting. Can't have him feeling excluded, now can we, Anna?' He was mocking now, on the attack again, and no wonder. 'See you next week.' Then he marched out, shutting the door firmly behind him.

Anna was so frenetic and prolific in the kitchen on Sunday that Jonathan found himself deluged with more goodies than ever. He wasn't complaining, he told Anna, eyeing her curiously, but he hoped she wasn't in danger of wearing herself, or her oven, out with all this

frenzied activity. She assured him it was all in the
interests of relaxing and recharging for the week ahead,
and he grunted and left it at that, only too happy to
help her dispose of the end product.

Before Monday's session, Anna was a mass of
tensions. The way she'd left things with Neil on
Thursday was bad enough, causing her all sorts of
anxieties and depressions she was usually immune to.
On a more objective level, she had already decided it
was time to take the plunge, to delve a bit deeper into
issues which might prove central in the case. Up to now
she had kept the sessions light and easygoing, steering
Neil away from reminders of anything too delicate or
painful for either brother. But this had only been a
preparation for the real work to come. Christopher
needed pushing harder if he was going to open up more.

Neil was briskly confident, showing no signs of
recalling their exchange of the previous week.
Christopher was his normal passive self, though Anna
was sure the impenetrable mask was beginning to lift.
She started them off on a safely impersonal note,
getting Neil to tell them about his time as an apprentice
cameraman in his late teens, then deftly introducing
Christopher's own early schooldays.

'You liked school, didn't you, Chris?' Neil fired the
direct question at his brother as he often did,
instinctively hoping that eventually one would produce
a direct answer. 'You always liked it. They didn't send
you away, of course, like they did me—nor would they
have done, I reckon,' he mused, fighting back a clear
note of bitterness.

Anna glanced at him, but he was well under control.
Only her expert and concerned eye could have detected
the crease furrowing his brow, the tense lines tightening
his mouth, the proud erect set of his head. 'Did you
ever feel like leaving home again, Neil?' she demanded
suddenly. 'You must have been—what—twenty-two
when Chris started proper school? And still living in the
family home?'

It was a challenge, almost an accusation, and he rose

to it. 'Why should I have wanted to leave? I wasn't exactly in their pockets,' he pointed out gruffly. 'It was—is—an enormous house. I saw no reason to move out when I had a whole floor to myself, company I liked when I wanted it but privacy when I didn't, all mod cons ...'

But Anna was on to a point, and she persisted. 'You never felt like getting out on your own, away from their protection—or perhaps their limitations?'

'My job took me away increasingly often,' Neil retorted, irritated now. 'I was only too glad to come home to a warm welcome, and why not?' he growled. 'Anyway, Chris wouldn't have wanted me to leave, would you, Chris?'

This time he addressed the query to his brother automatically, without even looking at him, still fiercely confronting Anna, the boy temporarily forgotten.

'No,' said Christopher firmly.

'See?' Neil was still facing Anna; but then the full impact of what had just happened hit him, and he swung round to stare at Christopher. The boy was pale but perfectly composed. 'No,' he repeated in his hoarse adolescent croak. 'It was good having you there. I didn't want you to leave.'

Anna, who had been hoping for just this, smiled at Christopher; and then she smiled at Neil, whose face was a study in astonishment. Another watershed, another breakthrough—but this was just the moment to press on, not rest on their laurels. 'Did you enjoy doing things together, as a family—all of you?' She was calm and level, as if nothing new had taken place.

Neil recovered his composure but Anna could tell he was still shaken. 'Yes, we quite often went out together at weekends, when I was at home. Then we always went on holiday in the summer ...' His voice faded away, and his eyes took on a vaguely stony expression, failing to meet hers.

Anna was immediately on her guard. 'Where did you go?'

'We had a cottage on the Isle of Wight.' Neil was

becoming more and more remote and withdrawn,
almost as if Christopher's sudden burst of communication had reversed their roles.

'That's great. I like the Isle of Wight. What did you
do there?'

Anna had never seen Neil so strung up. 'Oh,
swimming, snorkelling, all the usual kinds of things . . .'
He was having difficulty just getting the words out.

Christopher cleared his throat and sat up straight,
drawing their attention. Then he announced, staring
stiffly ahead, 'And sailing.'

Something in his tone alerted Anna even further. She
scented complications, something near the bone. Unless
she miscalculated, they were about to enter her new,
demanding territory. 'Sailing?' she echoed brightly. 'I've
never done it, must be lovely. What kind of boat?'

Neil had fallen bleakly silent, head bent down so that
Anna couldn't make out his expression. But Christopher,
by contrast, waxed positively eloquent. 'We had a
ketch—thirty foot—and a dinghy. Actually Mum and
Dad had the ketch, and the little one was Neil's. I used to
go in both,' he told her, not looking at Neil.

Anna decided to concentrate her energy on encouraging Christopher now he'd finally gone into
action, but it was impossible to ignore the anguished
vibrations which reached her from Neil. 'Which did you
like best?'

'Neither.' He shrugged. 'Both.' He stared through the
window, apparently exhausted by this intense effort to
communicate.

'And do you still go sailing? Have you still got the
place, or the yachts?'

'No.' All at once, Christopher turned to look straight
at Neil. 'We don't go there any more. We don't own the
cottage.'

Anna's intuition warned her the crunch was coming.
It was no use evading it: they had to reach it sooner or
later. 'Why not?' she asked, very softly. 'Neil? Chris?'
she prompted, after several seconds' complete silence.

Then, finding a reserve of strength, Neil lifted his

head to look full at her, his blue eyes blazing with a fierce emotion she had never seen in him. It was alarming, but Anna was used to controlling her own responses and all her training and skill came into play now. She simply looked back into his eyes, patiently waiting.

'It was sold.' Neil's voice was flat, dangerously toneless. 'When our parents died.'

'Why?' Anna knew this had to be followed through at all costs.

There was another long pause. Then Neil said, still in the same blank tone, 'They died there—drowned. Off the coast near Bembridge.'

'How awful! I'm so sorry!' Sincere sympathy, a poignant sense of their loss mingled with Anna's professional instinct to force them through this terrible patch. 'How did it happen?'

'They were in the dinghy.' Neil almost choked on his own words. Anna could only admire his ability to keep going at all. 'It capsized. They were never found.'

Not even a proper farewell, a burial, to take the edge off the pain! No wonder the two of them were so deeply traumatised, Anna thought. 'But weren't they experienced sailors? I thought you said . . .'

'They were experienced with the ketch, yes. They rarely went out in my dinghy. Anyway, the weather . . .' Neil broke off, his face contorting in the grip of a private agony. He had to go through it, and she had to witness it: both of them, at some level, knew that.

Anna turned to see how Christopher was taking this rough passage. To her sheer amazement, he was staring at his brother—and tears were cascading down his cheeks. Floods and rivulets of them, as if overflowing from a brimming tank. Silently, strangely, without sobs or gasps or sighs, Christopher Tyrell was weeping out some of his internal sorrow at last.

Because he was making no sound, Neil hadn't noticed Christopher's dramatic collapse. Clenching his fists, summoning up another shot of determination, he pressed grimly on. 'There was a storm,' he blurted.

'I see, Neil.' Anna was very quiet and poised, very soothing. Christopher went on weeping, and she reached in her bag for a clean handkerchief and offered it to him without a word. Without a word he reached out and took it, mopping his face and then clutching it like a lifeline while the tears continued to flow. Knowing she had to, Anna went on pushing. 'Where were you at the time?'

'Safely back at the cottage. We'd watched them through the window—sailing round the promontory and out of the bay . . .' Neil's tone registered a dull but deep anger now, probably directed at himself.

'Did the storm come up very suddenly?' she wondered, still calm and steady.

'Oh yes.' Neil was on his feet in one jerky movement, glaring down at his two companions. Whether he took in the fact that Christopher was crying, Anna could not be sure. His own face was savagely twisted as he relived those dreadful memories after avoiding them for so long. 'It came up suddenly all right. No warning, to speak of. Nothing could have been done,' he barked. 'Not a bloody thing!'

Anna resisted the urge to stand up as well, reminding herself that Christopher was the main point of this exercise, and he was still sitting, rigid and weeping, in his chair. 'Neil . . .' She held out a hand to him, her instinct to comfort briefly overpowering her professional distance. 'It's all right. There was nothing . . .'

But he paid no attention to her, lost in his own suffering. *'Not a bloody thing!'* he shouted again, as if someone had contradicted him. Then, to her consternation, he swung round on his heel and marched from the room.

Anna turned back to Christopher, whose tears were abating almost as instantly as they had started, and who was now staring after his brother with an air of puzzled anxiety. Somewhere behind it, there lurked a new stability. 'Don't worry, Chris.' Anna leaned over to lay a gentle hand on his arm. 'He'll be fine in a minute.'

Christopher regarded her solemnly, then he shook his

head and handed her back the soggy handkerchief. 'It was an accident, Anna,' he stated, like one adult discussing a wayward child with another. 'The wind caught them and took them over.'

Anna pulled a wry face and shook her head back at him. She hardly knew whether to feel exalted or appalled by this unexpected climax to the session. A few minutes later she sent Christopher off, telling him to wait for Neil in reception. The hour wasn't quite up but it had, she decided, served its purpose. Anyway, never mind the two Tyrells, Anna was pretty worn out herself.

Neil never returned to her room. Anna spent the next two days in a state of high suspense. She had engineered this emotional breakthrough, but would he see it as a shameful collapse? How was he feeling now: painfully exposed, bitter—or relieved? There was no way of finding out until Thursday.

Meanwhile, how did she feel, in herself? This was a question which normally had no place in her working life: after all, she was well used to such fireworks. They were a necessary part of the process she was continually orchestrating. But in this case, she had to face it, everything that happened to the clients seemed to have its direct impact on her. Her involvement with these people—or rather, if she was honest, with Neil—was something unprecedented, unique. She could never be sure what the next step would bring; and this uncertainty was a whole new experience.

Thursday arrived, eventually; but this time Neil failed her. Christopher duly turned up, loping in and sitting down as if nothing had happened. But he was alone. Anna's professional disappointment was brief and soon over; but not the sharp pain of personal loss which grew from it and swelled to fill the space it left. She had come to depend on Neil's presence, there in her room, twice a week.

But it was more than her job was worth to let Christopher know that. 'Hallo, Chris!' she greeted him with forced cheeriness. 'All on your own today?'

She had grown so used to not expecting replies to her

conversational queries that she almost jumped when he answered, quite naturally, 'Neil wouldn't come.'

'Wouldn't?'

'He said he wasn't going to . . .' he frowned, recalling his brother's exact words, '. . . to sit there and be dissected into little pieces.'

'Oh.' This was a severe blow, but she took it on the chin. 'Never mind,' she said brightly, 'we'll have to manage without him, won't we?'

But they did not really manage without Neil at all. Without him it was more or less pointless. It had been his presence which had sparked off Christopher's emotional release; and his presence was vital if it was to happen again, which it needed to several times yet.

Anna refused to give up of course; taking Christopher over the key event again, then moving on to other aspects of it, making an attempt to probe his true feelings. But the boy remained impassive, polite but bland, refusing to come out from behind his screen just for her benefit. The interaction was between the two brothers; Anna was merely the agent, the medium through whom it took place. Without Neil there was no communication, just an empty, cautious, rattling of words. At least Christopher did murmur the odd verbal response now, but mostly Anna fired questions which he dodged or evaded.

Afterwards she felt more profoundly drained than she had been on Monday. Then, there had at least been a sense of achievement. Today it was just static—stagnant. 'Is Neil coming for you?' she enquired wearily, walking over to her desk.

'No. I can get home on my own.'

'Are you sure, Chris?' She looked at him doubtfully.

'Of course I'm sure.' He slouched to the door, scornful. 'I got here all right, didn't I? It's only a short bus ride. I've done it loads of times. I'm not a kid you know, Anna.' His spirit was returning along with his confidence. That was good—but there was a long way to go yet, and they couldn't get there without Neil.

'No, Chris, you're not a kid. I'm sorry. See you on

Monday, then? And Chris—try and persuade Neil to come back,' she implored, but without much hope.

'Yeah, I will,' he assured her with unexpected vehemence. Obviously he wanted Neil there as much as she did. 'But I might not see him much; he said he was away this weekend.' So, Christopher was emerging from his self-imposed prison, too, was he? Things were certainly shifting. What a pity if she had to lose one brother as a price for restoring the other!

Neil did not come at all the next week. Anna held out through both sessions, to make sure they really weren't getting anywhere without him. Christopher remained reasonable and forthcoming—certainly not the morosely dumb creature he had been at first—but they made no progress because he simply wouldn't, or couldn't, let out any real feelings. Each time, Anna asked him if he had tried to get Neil to come, and each time he said the same.

'I tried, yeah, but he won't come back. Says it's all too heavy and I'm better enough already. We don't need him any more, he says.'

'And do you agree?'

He shrugged, staring into the distance. 'Don't know. No, not really.'

No. Christopher knew as well as she did that the first breakthrough was not the same as final success.

On Friday evening, Anna finally gave way to professional and personal despair. Before she left the clinic, she mustered all her courage and telephoned Neil.

'Neil? This is Anna Coleman,' she told him stiffly.

'Anna!' His greeting contained more open pleasure than hers. 'Good to hear you!'

'Is it?' she countered suspiciously.

'Sure, why not? What can I do for you?'

She bristled at his studied chirpiness. 'You know perfectly well what you can do for me, Neil. You can condescend to rejoin our sessions.'

'I'd do a lot for you, Anna,' he retorted, more like his old sardonic self, 'but I'm not doing that. Sorry.'

'But, Neil, why?' She forced herself to sound persuasive rather than frustrated. 'I know things got a bit—difficult last time you came, but I did warn you we had to go through sticky patches before . . .'

'Anna,' he interrupted curtly. 'I meant what I said. Sorry. It's just too much.'

'But, Neil . . .'

'Look, Chris is really on the mend now, isn't he? I can't deny your methods have paid off. He even comes down to meals, we even get a few words out of him now and then. Things are looking up.'

'But he's far from his old self yet, surely?' she insisted. 'Anyway, he's only showing this improvement *because* of your involvement. If you give up now . . .'

'I apologise if it seems like giving up,' Neil cut in brusquely. 'But I can't cope with any more, Anna. I'm sorry.'

'It does seem like giving up,' she confirmed drily. 'That's exactly what it is.'

'He cried last time,' Neil reminded her, obviously hating even to think about it.

'Yes, he cried. And it was one of the best things that could have happened. A really major development, which you helped to . . .'

'I'd rather not be in on any more major developments, if you don't mind, Anna. Spewing out all this misery and hostility—and not only his,' he added, touching on the real raw point. '*I* don't intend to be turned inside out, or to occupy a ringside seat while he is, either. You do your job, and leave me to help Chris as best I can here, at this end. Okay?'

'No, Neil, it's not okay.' If he could be stubborn, so could she. 'You can't just back out like this. You said you'd help, and you've been doing it so well . . .'

'Flattery will get you nowhere,' he mocked infuriatingly.

Anna schooled herself into patience yet again. This was like retracing tired old ground which she had thought they'd left long behind. 'Isn't there anything I can say or do to make you change your mind?' she pleaded.

There was a short pregnant pause before Neil demanded, 'Such as?'

'Well, you could talk it over with one of my colleagues. Daniel Davidson would confirm what I'm telling you about how important it is,' she suggested, rather breathlessly. 'Or even if you'd only come once a week it might be something.'

'No. I'll take your word for it, and I'm sure I'd take theirs. But I'm not coming back, Anna.' He was unbending; programmed.

'Look, Neil—it won't always be so . . . I don't have to get you to talk about your parents' death any more. Or anything that painful. Though I do think,' she added boldly, honesty forcing its way out, 'that you should. You've got an even bigger block about it than Christopher has.'

Now there was anger behind the rockface of obstinacy. 'I dare say I have. I'll take your word for that, too. Sorry, Anna. No more—no way.'

The line hummed with silence, while she drummed her fingers on the desk in annoyance. Then, suddenly, she'd had it up to here; nothing, no one, no case was worth this much grovelling and wheedling. 'Right then. I'll keep in touch—let you know how it goes, officially. Thanks for doing what you did, anyway.'

This reversal of tactics had an unexpected effect (or perhaps, in the back of her mind, she had half been expecting it?). Neil's voice came back to her, softened slightly, shot through with challenge. 'I have got one suggestion, Anna: a sort of compromise we might reach.'

'Oh yes?' It was her turn to be cool and cautious, defensive.

'If we were to meet somewhere neutral—outside the Unit—away from all that clinical formality. Where we could be on equal terms.'

'But we are on equal terms! We're not in the least formal . . .!'

'Not the way I see it,' he denied. 'I feel constrained, hamstrung in that place.'

'But it isn't even ethical for me to see you privately

while the case is going on! I'm not supposed to . . .' Her voice rose to a shrill screech, quite out of character, in her alarm. His unorthodox proposition had completely turned the tables on her, catching her squarely on the soft underbelly.

'Look, Anna, you asked what you could do to make me change my mind. Well, this is the only thing I can think of. Who knows—if you approach me in person . . . in the flesh,' he paraphrased pointedly, causing her skin to redden and tingle, 'I might be able to tell you more than I can when we're all stuck in your room. You might even,' he observed enticingly, 'change my mind and get me to come back.'

She fought down a wave of panic at the prospect. Neil Tyrell seemed to have a direct line to her body, bypassing her brain, even from the other end of an impersonal machine. 'But you don't understand, Neil: Chris needs you at the sessions! You and I together, somewhere else, without him, wouldn't be any use at all!'

'On the contrary,' he drawled, sardonic again now. 'I think we'd be very useful indeed. Anyway, it's my last offer. Meet me somewhere else, and I'll reconsider.'

'But that's blackmail!' Anna was outraged, and at the same time curiously excited.

'I wouldn't put it quite as strongly as that,' he protested mildly; but she could tell from his tone that he knew he had gained the upper hand.

Her brain and blood were racing, for once equally charged. What should she do? She really cared, her brain told her, about this case. If this was the only way to reinstate Neil on it, shouldn't she agree? But then, her blood reminded her uncomfortably, she cared about the man, too. Wouldn't it be the most appalling risk, meeting him outside the safe confines of the clinic, on neutral ground? Damn the conflicts he was setting up! Damn him, and his complications, and the ones he was creating for her! Damn the two of them, undermining her certainty, depleting her precious confidence . . .

'Are you still there, Anna?' he drawled. 'Reached a decision yet?'

'What did you have in mind?' she prevaricated warily.

'Oh, just a spot of lunch. Nothing too compromising,' he teased.

Anna squared her shoulders and came to a conclusion. 'Okay, Neil. I'll meet you for lunch. If you feel there might be things you could say in that setting which you can't tell me in my consulting room, I'll have lunch with you—once. But what I really want,' she reminded him sternly, 'is to get you back in here with Chris. As long as that's understood?'

'Understood, Dr C. So, when? How about this weekend?'

'No, I'd prefer a weekday,' she said firmly. There was something comfortingly routine about a weekday lunch. 'It had better not be one of Christopher's days ... let me see ... can we say Tuesday? I can take two hours off then, I don't have a client until three. I usually keep that hour for catching up on notes. I can be ready at one,' she told him briskly.

'One o'clock Tuesday. I'll pick you up.'

'I'm quite capable of driving myself somewhere,' she pointed out in starchy tones.

'I realise that, but I don't know where I'm taking you yet,' he returned blandly.

She could clearly picture the spark of triumph which was surely glittering in his eyes. He might have scored a petty victory, but he need not think he could start calling the tune. She was simply giving way in a minor skirmish in order to win a major battle of wills. It took greater willpower, she told herself, to concede a point gracefully.

'Okay, Neil. I'll be ready,' she agreed meekly. *Softly, softly, catchee monkey*, one of her tutors at college used to advise cryptically. In this case, Anna reflected as she replaced the receiver, it was very apt.

She only wished she could be more certain which of them was doing the catching.

CHAPTER FIVE

BEFORE she left work on Monday, Anna found herself
knocking on the door to Daniel's consulting room and
then confronting him across his desk. He greeted her
with his usual broad grin. 'Hallo there, Anna. How's it
going? Good weekend? Do anything nice?' he wondered
hopefully, drawing his bushy brows together.

'Nothing special. Daniel, I . . .'

'We enjoyed having you over the other week. Muriel
was saying so only yesterday. You must come again
soon; we'd all like it if you did.'

'Thanks, Daniel. I'd really love to. I enjoyed it too.
Aren't the little ones growing? That Benjamin's a real
pickle, isn't he?' Momentarily sidetracked, Anna smiled
as she remembered the antics of Daniel's youngest
grandchild.

'Shocking,' agreed Daniel fondly. 'And his sister's no
better.'

'Anyway, what I came to say was . . .'

'Are you worrying about anything, Anna?' he
interrupted again, beetling at her in concern. 'You've
been looking a bit tired lately.'

'Not particularly,' she retorted at once. 'Things have
been a bit hectic, but . . .'

'How's the Tyrell case working out?' Daniel never
missed a trick, Anna reflected ruefully. 'I've had a quick
look at the file; I noticed the brother attended a few
therapy sessions but then opted out—why was that?'

'That's why I'm here.' Anna tried again, then waited
to make sure he wasn't going to interrupt a third time.
When he didn't, she took a deep breath and went on.
'The case is going badly, Daniel. To be accurate, it isn't
really going at all. While Neil was there we made some
very real progress, but then he lost his nerve and just
gave up. Since then, Christopher and I have been stuck

on one of those plateaux—you know—we just go round in circles. I try to make contact and he behaves like a prey being stalked. We talk, which is more than we did; but we don't *move* anywhere.' She sighed. 'I had him again today. He's friendly enough—quite forthcoming really, in a polite sort of way—less unhappy than he was, I suppose; but still locked away. It was only with his brother there that he began to let things out. We made one major breakthrough, as you'll have seen in the notes, but then it was Neil who seemed to undergo a crisis, even more than Christopher. He stormed out and then declared he wasn't coming back. I've tried seeing the boy on his own, several times, but it's useless, so . . .'

'Have you tried getting Neil to come back? 'Phoning, writing?' Daniel leaned forward on his desk, watching Anna intently.

'Yes, of course. I sent messages with Chris: he's just as keen on having Neil involved as I am. Then last week, I 'phoned.'

'Still no go?' Daniel was sympathetic.

'No. Well, at least . . .'

'Did he say why? What made him give up?'

'He said the whole thing was too—what was his word?—heavy. He does want to help, but he can't cope with doing it this way. I suppose he never really accepted the idea right from the start. Last year.' She paused, her memory drifting back; then she faced Daniel again. 'But he did say he might change his mind—if . . .'

'If what?' Daniel prompted eagerly as she tailed off again.

'If I see him outside the Unit. Away from this clinical atmosphere, he said.'

Daniel was intrigued. 'How do you mean, Anna—see him?' He studied her more shrewdly than ever, and she wished he wouldn't.

'Well, you know—socially. Meet him for lunch, kind of thing. Talk about the case, of course; and I get the impression there might be something he wants to say which can't be said here, in this context, for some reason. Some private block, I don't know.' She shrugged, as nonchalantly as possible.

'And what did you say?' Daniel pressed, when she came to a halt once more.

'I didn't want to, Daniel. It's against all the rules, and . . .'

'What rules?' he cut in sharply.

'Well, you know, professional etiquette . . .'

'Damn all that! If this is how you save a case, then this is what you have to do.' Anna stared at him as he banged one hand on his desk to emphasise his point. 'You know what I think, Anna: play it by ear, feel your way through. No two cases are ever the same,' he reminded her, more gently. 'It's no good making hard rules. As long as you're discreet, which you always are. After all,' he pointed out, 'it's not as if Tyrell himself was the client: that might be different. He's only family.'

'Yes, well.' Anna knew all that, of course, but she could hardly explain to Daniel that it was her own, much deeper rules which really felt threatened by Neil's proposition. 'I said I would. I came to check with you that you think it's all right if I meet him for lunch tomorrow.' There, it was said at last.

Daniel grinned. 'Took you long enough to spit it out, didn't it?'

'You kept butting in!' she defended herself heatedly.

'I did, I did,' he soothed. 'You're absolutely right. I'm a verbose old . . .' Without batting an eyelid, Daniel described himself in graphic terms which would have astonished his young clients. 'Never let you get a word in edgeways. Well, Anna, if you came to unburden your conscience about this decision on to me, please consider it done. I endorse it one hundred per cent, and I wish you all the best.' Was she imagining it, or was there the faintest gleam in his eye? 'Keep this chap in order; get him back into the fold, eh? You can do it. Let me know how it goes.'

'It's only a quick business lunch,' she told him stiffly. 'I dare say we'll go to a snack bar, or Macdonalds, or somewhere totally prosaic, and I'll listen to whatever it is he can't say here, and then tell him if he doesn't come back he can't expect Christopher to make any more progress. That's all.'

'It sounds more than enough to me,' Daniel said gravely. 'Good luck anyway.'

'Thanks.' Five minutes later, as she climbed into her car, Anna realised she had been half—more than half—hoping Daniel would veto the whole idea. Well, she lectured herself, catching her reflection with a wry smile in the driving mirror, if that had been her unconscious motivation in consulting her colleague, it had certainly backfired on her in a big way.

Neil's Rover was waiting outside the clinic when Anna emerged at one o'clock next day, hands in the pockets of her long knitted jacket—there was quite a chilly wind for late spring—and bag slung across her shoulder. She had taken care to dress even more informally than usual, in cord jeans and a simple blouse; she had no intention of letting the man think she'd got herself up on his account.

He reached over to open the passenger door as she approached. Climbing into the plush front seat and pulling the door shut, Anna noted with relief that Neil was no smarter than she was. Clearly, in those routine denims and the plain black sweater, he wasn't planning to drag her off to some fancy restaurant, showing her up, dazzling her into forgetting just what this was all about—because if he had any notions like that, he could . . .

'Good afternoon!' Anna coloured, realising he was addressing her politely and she'd been too carried away in her private resentments even to notice. 'On the dot,' he remarked as he started up the engine, 'but then I'd have expected no less.'

He flashed her a smile that was courteous and charming, but superficial. Then he got on with the business of manoeuvring the sleek car out into the road. Anna wasn't sure what she had been expecting, but somehow this blandness was strangely disconcerting. 'Hallo, Neil,' she returned briskly. 'Where are we going?'

He was now negotiating the traffic on the dual carriageway with the confident air of a man quite sure of his destination. 'Wait and see,' he advised irritatingly. 'It's not far,' he added, as if to reassure her.

'It had better not be,' she grumbled. 'I told you I haven't got too long. I hope it's nowhere too up-market, either,' she warned, 'because I'm not in the mood, nor the right gear, for . . .'

'Oh, don't worry, it's not at all posh.' He changed down gear smoothly as they drew up to a red light. 'It's a little place I know very well indeed.' He turned to smile at her again, hands resting on the steering wheel as the big car throbbed quietly in the queue. 'Now Anna—would I subject you to anywhere, or anything, I knew you wouldn't like?'

Anna restrained herself to a non-committal grunt. She seemed to be feeling unusually edgy and barbed today, perhaps because she disliked not being in total control of her situation. Neil, on the other hand, was as cool and unconcerned as she'd yet seen him; no doubt because he was off her territory and, for the moment at least, in charge. He whistled softly through his teeth as he left the busy highway and turned off round the back, among the dignified squares and residential terraced rows that characterise Canonbury, one of the most expensive parts of the borough.

'How the other half lives,' Anna observed caustically, gazing out at a particularly elegant crescent into which he had just swung the car.

'I thought you said you lived in Islington, too?' Neil checked in his rear view mirror before pulling up in a space marked 'permit holders only', just outside the end house: tall, graceful, early Victorian, facing on to a view of the peaceful little green plot inside the crescent, now brightened by a magnificent show of tulips and some blossoming ornamental cherry trees.

'Oh, I do; but definitely not this Islington. The grotty

end, near Archway. Not quite in this class, Neil.' Anna was looking about her with a growing unease, bordering on paranoia. 'There can't be many eating places here—not the kind I had in mind? Couldn't we just have gone to one of the ordinary cafés near the . . .?'

'On the contrary,' he corrected her calmly, removing the keys from the ignition and then coming round to open her door from the outside. 'This is one of the best eateries for miles,' he announced, escorting her out of the car with a flourish. 'I should know, because I live here!'

Anna glared up at him, a study in outrage. Her suspicions had been more than justified: bringing her to his own house, indeed! She should have listened to those instinctive signals, insisted on driving herself somewhere . . . and now it was too late; short of making herself look a complete idiot, she could hardly refuse point blank to come in.

'Are we going to stand here all afternoon?' he enquired pleasantly, 'or shall we go in and find some lunch? Mrs R will be waiting for us.'

Ah yes, of course—the efficient housekeeper! Well, at least they would not be on their own; there was some comfort in that thought. Anna stared up at the mellow beauty of the house, then round at its equally fine neighbours. Shaking her dark head in resignation, she turned to confront Neil, a spark of battle in her eyes. 'This was a dirty trick, Neil! You know I wasn't expecting to come here!'

He shrugged, allowing his blue eyes to wander lazily over her face. 'It's so near, it seemed the most convenient way. Why not?'

'But you could have warned me!' she protested, her gaze still reluctantly drawn to admire the stately grandeur of the place. It was impossible not to relish such a tranquil, timeless oasis so near the scrum of the great city.

'And if I'd issued a formal invitation,' he challenged, bending down to lock the car and then setting off towards the front steps, 'would you have accepted, with grateful thanks?'

'No,' she admitted, aware of a rising tension inside her as she followed him.

'Well then—Q.E.D.—my case rests.' At the door he turned to face her before putting his key in the lock. The studied blandness had given way to a more familiar forceful irony. 'So far, Anna, you've called the tune. We've been on your patch, in your time, for your reasons, at your instigation. Now it's my turn to entertain you,' he informed her decisively.

'I didn't agree to meet you today in order to be *entertained*!' she snapped, instantly resentful of his attitude.

He smiled briefly; then he opened the door and preceded her into a lofty hall, carefully furnished and decorated to enhance its period flavour. 'I realise that,' he acknowledged quietly. 'You and I have important matters to discuss, but I thought we could do it here as well as anywhere else—and much more comfortably.'

Looking round now, Anna could hardly deny that this was true. She opened her mouth to reply sharply, but then closed it again when she saw they were no longer alone. A handsome middle-aged woman, her lively face lit up by a warm smile of welcome, had emerged—presumably from the kitchen regions, Anna thought drily—and was holding out her hand. 'Dr Coleman? How do you do? I've heard so much about you!'

The greeting was so genuinely friendly, Anna could only take the offered hand and smile back. 'How do you do: Mrs Robertson, isn't it?' she murmured, suddenly shy. On her own ground Anna was always in charge; socially she was reticent.

Neil was surveying her with an expression of interested amusement which she found infuriating. 'Yes, this is our guardian angel, Mrs R. I told you about her.'

'Of course you did.' Anna recovered her poise, and her smile became more natural, radiating her face with spontaneous charm which caused the older woman to look at her in pleased surprise. 'Very kind of you to have me to lunch,' she found herself saying warmly.

Mrs R laughed happily. 'It's Neil who issues the invitations. I just make the lunch,' she remarked, with a hint of satire.

'Lucky Neil!' Anna couldn't resist the dig, but Mrs R only laughed again. It was clear, even on such short acquaintance, that she was far from the inadequate, uninvolved influence Anna had feared. Her attitude to Neil, and no doubt even more to Christopher, was motherly and affectionate.

'Oh, he can manage perfectly well for himself when he has to, don't you worry about that. I do get time off, you know.' She gazed at Neil fondly. 'He's quite a dab hand in the kitchen, between you and me, Dr Coleman.'

'I'm sure he is.' Anna glanced at Neil, who was grinning openly.

'I heat up a tasty baked bean,' he proclaimed, 'and scramble a mean egg. Chris is better at it than me, though. Mrs R's seen to that. She believes in equality of the sexes, and ever since she's been in charge he's had to do his share.'

'I'm glad to hear it.' Anna's opinion of Mrs R rose even higher.

'Till recently, of course,' the housekeeper sighed, her eyes filming with anxiety.

'Where is Christopher? Will he be eating with us?' Anna asked, looking round.

'Oh no—he's in his room. He's already had a snack up there,' Mrs R said.

'He still spends most of the day lurking in his den,' Neil explained, his face momentarily grim. 'Nothing short of fire or earthquake is likely to shake him out. Anyway,' he pointed out, rather aggressively, 'we don't want him here, do we? The general idea is for you and me to have a private chat—isn't it?'

'That *was* the general idea, yes.' Anna's tone suggested that things had already strayed a long way from what she'd originally considered the general idea. 'But I'm sorry to hear he's still shutting himself away; I

thought he was coming down to meals now?' She
turned to Mrs R, her expression registering concern for
the boy.

'Oh, he'll be down for supper,' Mrs R assured her.
'We insist on it, if nothing else, don't we, Neil?'

'We certainly do.' Neil nodded vehemently. 'And he's
sometimes quite sociable, too, these days, compared to
a few months back.'

'In a stiff kind of way, yes; but he's still not really his
old self.' Mrs R shook her head sadly. It was obvious
she was as attached to Christopher as anyone would be
after years of caring for a child. Then she brightened.
'But he's ever so much better since he started coming to
you, Doctor.'

'I'm glad to hear that—but we've got a long way to
go yet,' Anna said quietly.

'And that's why you're here, of course, to talk it over
with Neil. And here I am, taking up your valuable time
with chat. What must you think of me?' she bustled.

'Not at all,' Anna contradicted politely. 'I'm sure
Neil thought meeting you was just as important as
talking to him.' The words were out almost before she'd
thought them through, but at once she recognised them
as a flash of insight. Neil had inveigled her here in order
to see their environment for herself, and that could only
help when it came to sorting out Christopher's
problems. Regrettably, he was quite right.

Mrs R beamed, delighted. 'Well, you'll be wanting to
get on with your dinner. I've left it all ready—soup,
cheese and salad and some of my home-made rolls, as
you suggested, Neil. So if you don't mind, I'll be getting
off now.'

Anna's face expressed her dismay. 'Aren't you joining
us, then?'

'Oh no, dear, I've had mine; anyway, you won't want
me there during your private discussions.' Mrs R was
horrified at the very idea. 'And I've got a shopping list
as long as your arm.' She turned to Neil. 'I promised to
meet my sister at four, we thought we'd have tea at that
place near Upper Street, so if you don't mind . . .'

'Not a bit. We'll be fine. Thanks a lot, Mrs R.' Neil smiled at Anna. 'We'll manage unsupervised, won't we, Anna?'

Anna laughed mildly, as she knew she was supposed to. She knew when she was cornered; she might as well carry on giving in gracefully. Her time would come.

The simple lunch was laid out ready on a wooden table in the bright modern kitchen which contrived to be airy and spacious, yet cosy and enfolding at the same time. Anna, to whom kitchens were by far the most significant part of any house, had a job not to show how impressed she was. Neil knew nothing of her culinary activities, and probably never would; secretly, though, Anna admired and appreciated the tasty smoothness of Mrs R's soup, the even texture of her wholemeal bread.

Now she concentrated on buttering a roll. 'Well, this isn't quite the scene I was expecting,' she observed, her tone steady and light.

'I must say you're taking it remarkably well.' Neil poured out apple juice for them both: Anna had refused wine, protesting that she, at least, had to work this afternoon. 'Somehow I hadn't thought I'd get away with it so easily.'

She raised misleadingly limpid hazel eyes to gaze at him across the table. 'Get away with it?' she echoed innocently.

He chuckled. 'You know what I mean, Anna. After all, I did kidnap you—it wasn't exactly fighting fair. I wanted to get you here, to see how we live for yourself, and you've already admitted you'd never have come if I'd asked you straight.'

'Fighting fair?' Her dark brows arched delicately. 'I wasn't aware we were engaged in a fight at all,' she lied sweetly, spooning up some of the thick soup.

Neil chuckled again. 'You're a lady full of surprises, a law unto yourself, aren't you?' He bit into a roll, gazing at her reflectively. 'Maybe that's why I find you so fascinating.'

Her insides lurched at his words, but she kept her

outward cool. 'What you mean is, you find me a challenge.'

'Is that what I mean?' Neil paused, spoon halfway to his mouth.

'Well,' she elaborated carefully, 'I don't expect your dealings with women are usually conducted on quite this basis. We have a very specific and intricate relationship,' she pointed out honestly, 'but it's not personal, and it's not permanent, so it must be hard for you to fit it into whatever categories you normally put the women in your life. If Christopher's psychologist had been a man, you'd still have had some problems— but they might well have been different ones. As it is . . .'

'As it is,' he supplied, as she paused to sip her soup, 'my brother's shrink is most definitely not a man. I find myself confronting a person who may be brilliant at her job but is indisputably, exceedingly female.'

'Those two characteristics are not necessarily mutually exclusive,' Anna remarked.

'I never implied they were.' Neil looked surprised, then he grinned. 'I've got no wish to take on your job, flower, but I get the feeling you find it all just as difficult as I do, for all your wise understanding of these matters.'

'I find every tough case difficult,' Anna observed tautly, knowing exactly what he meant all the same, and wishing he was a lot less perceptive.

'And that's what makes you good at your work—you really get to the heart of things.' He leaned across the table towards her, only increasing her already powerful reaction to his presence. 'But you know that's not quite what I meant, Anna.'

Her stomach contracted, but she met his eyes steadily, determined not to show her feelings. 'Do I?'

She expected him to become irritable and thwarted, but he surprised her by taking a more serious tone, his eyes solemn and clear on hers. 'You were right just now, of course,' he confided, his very honesty confounding her. 'I was finding it dead tricky to deliver the goods in those sessions. I thought a lot about it, and I reached the conclusion it was because you're a woman.' He hesitated, smiling faintly as he searched for the right words. 'I've had plenty to do with women, as you surmise, at all sorts of levels and in many contexts. I enjoy their company. Minds,' he assured her mischievously, 'as well as bodies. But I've always avoided exposing my inner self to one, or making any emotional commitments.'

Anna calmly buttered another roll, but she was taking in every word avidly. 'Have you ever wondered why?' she mused lightly.

He shrugged. 'Of course. When Mother was alive, I was very close to her, perhaps too close to let other women in ... then when she died, none of them seemed ... I don't know ...' His expression set hard as he relived his personal loss for the umpteenth time. Then it broke into a grin of self-protection. 'I'm not ready to attach myself yet, Anna. Far too much fun to be had from all women, to limit myself to any one. I enjoy playing the field too much to give it up.' He waited to see whether she would rise to the bait, but she simply sat listening and watching as he talked. After all, she was the expert when it came to impassively receiving information, however gripping it might secretly be. Suddenly Neil added; 'And let's face it, Anna, you're not just any example of the gender: you're a particularly fine one. Is it any wonder I felt a bit confused, having to open up to you like that?'

This caught her off guard, definitely overstepping the mark. She stared down at her soup, successfully controlling the blush which threatened to suffuse her. Once she was sure of herself, she looked up. 'I realise how difficult it was for you, Neil. But I have tried to explain: if you could only overcome these personal defence mechanisms, for Christopher's sake ...'

'Oh, I know all about that!' He dismissed her persuasions with a wave of his spoon. 'You can spare us both all that stuff today; you've made your position crystal clear. I know you think it's me you've come here to talk about, but you're missing my point.'

'What point?' This time Anna was genuinely puzzled.

'I was simply trying to suggest,' he explained slowly, 'that if I felt like that because you're a woman, isn't it more than likely that you'll find an extra dimension of conflict in our case because I'm a man?'

This was too near the truth for comfort or safety, and Anna almost physically dodged it. 'But at least half of my clients are male,' she exclaimed heatedly, 'not to mention their relatives!'

He grunted, taking refuge behind irony. 'Oh sure. Half the human race is male. That's not what I was getting at, and you know it.' He shrugged. 'Still, it's not my place to dig around in people's heads; I leave that to the experts. I was only trying to put my finger on whatever's making things so tense between us.'

'I hadn't noticed,' she claimed, 'that things were unduly tense between us.'

He was silent, helping himself to salad. When he looked up, his expression was deeply quizzical. 'You hadn't,' he repeated thoughtfully. Then, disarmingly, he grinned widely. 'Then it must be just me,' he declared lightly, picking up his knife and fork.

Anna was only too relieved to let that subject go, and for a while they both concentrated on eating Mrs R's delicious green salad. Eventually Anna tried a new tack. 'Is there something else you wanted to say to me?' she ventured.

Neil glanced up sharply, pushed on to the defensive. 'Something else?'

'Well, you reacted so strongly when we got to the bit about your parents' death,' Anna pressed gently, regaining the upper hand, 'I wondered if there were things you felt or remembered which you couldn't say in front of Christopher, or in that setting. Isn't that why you were so keen to get me away from it?' she reminded him.

'I asked you to meet me, and brought you here, for just two reasons.' Now it was Neil's turn to be gruffly unhelpful. 'First, as I've already told you, I wanted to get you on to my own territory. Second, as I've already tried to do, I wanted to tell you why I was finding the sessions so impossible, and why I can't come back.'

'Neil, I wasn't born yesterday. I know there's more to it than that.' Anna finished her salad and sat back, her eyes on his face. 'You were really bowling along for a while. I have to confess I was amazed—and impressed,' she admitted with endearing candour. 'Then suddenly— pow!' She slammed a fist into an open palm to illustrate the impact of the moment. 'There was this insurmountable block. You changed into a different creature. End of sessions.'

Neil pushed back his chair and ran agitated fingers through his thick fair hair, as he often did at times of stress or uncertainty. 'It all got too much for me.'

'But why did it get too much just then—at that exact juncture?' Unwilling to let a crucial moment go, Anna leaned forward, keen and persistent.

'What else would you expect?' Neil's face darkened, his eyes became hooded. 'We were discussing the death of my own parents in a horrible drowning accident— not one of my favourite subjects for dissection,' he grated sarcastically. 'Surely, in your trade, you come across plenty of people who get hung up on things like that?'

'Of course I do, Neil,' she assured him quietly, 'but you're not even the client, you're his nearest relative, and yet you seem to have an emotional block even more . . .'

'For Christ's sake, woman!' All at once he was on his feet, looming above her. 'Once and for all, will you give over talking in jargon? It's not a "block"—it's a perfectly normal reluctance to be forced through painful memories, that's all! I'm no good at it; you'll have to help Chris some other way. Now, could we please drop the subject?' With an effort he controlled himself, but his hands still gripped the back of his chair as he stood behind it. 'I shall make us some coffee, and we shall take it in the sitting room in a civilised manner.'

Anna stared at him for a moment, then gave up. All this ducking and dodging wasn't getting them anywhere. In their own ways, in good faith, they were both doing their best to tackle the problem of how to get Neil to help Christopher; but for the moment, it seemed, they had stumbled up against a classic impasse.

The sitting room was calm and tasteful, but no less comfortably warm than the kitchen. Anna looked round in appreciation before sitting on one of the two sofas. 'This is a nice room, Neil. Do you take care of all the decorating and everything, or does Mrs R choose, or what?'

He set the coffee tray down on a low table. 'Basically my choice, but Mrs R takes the executive action. I'm away too often to see to maintenance and that sort of thing. She keeps all major decisions for me, but mostly she's very competent.'

Anna had forgotten how rare it must be for Neil to be at home for so long at a time. It was only because of Christopher's problems that he was taking such an extended break between freelance assignments. 'What's your next project?' She was only partly making conversation: his work genuinely intrigued her.

He sat beside her on the sofa, handing her a cup of coffee. 'It's funny you should ask me that. I wanted to consult you about it.'

'Oh yes?' Anna took the cup and sipped the dark strong brew. 'I can't think what I could possibly have to say. I hardly even watch television, let alone . . .'

'No, so you said.' Neil relaxed, stretching out his legs in front of him, apparently unaware of the fact that this brought one of them into close contact with one of hers. Anna wished she could be half so immune. 'So you've never seen one of my creations?'

'I don't think so.' Anna's voice was taut and thin; she hoped Neil had not noticed how tense she had suddenly become. She couldn't move away so that they no longer touched: that would be too obvious. She'd just have to sit it out. 'Sorry.' She made a rather unsuccessful attempt at a careless smile.

'Not to worry—you haven't missed much.' He drank his coffee, then put the cup down on the table. There was a short pause while Anna did the same. Then she glanced self-consciously at her watch.

'It's two-twenty!' she exclaimed, with forced brightness. 'I must think about . . .'

'Nonsense,' he cut in. 'I can have you back in harness within ten minutes. You can stay another quarter of an hour yet, at least.'

'Well . . .' She was inexplicably anxious, all of a sudden, to escape from his sphere of influence.

'Anyway,' he reminded her, 'I haven't consulted you yet.'

Anna's mind had gone blank; and somehow Neil was getting nearer, one long arm now reaching round to lie nonchalantly along the back of the sofa, behind her shoulders. 'Consulted me?' she croaked, her voice unaccountably husky.

'About my next film,' he elucidated, smiling down at her.

'I still don't quite see . . .' Unconsciously she had twisted her hands tightly together in her lap, and was staring down at them.

'Anna.' He laid a cool hand over her writhing fingers. 'You've gone all uptight. What's the matter?'

'Matter?' she squeaked helplessly. 'Nothing—why?'

'You don't get like this,' he accused, very softly, 'in your consulting room.'

'Like what?' She knew she ought to struggle, complain, stand up and walk away; but she was trapped, caught in a web of sensation and reaction which had no place in her vocabulary of experience.

'Out of your depth. I've never seen you out of control of a situation,' he mused, his voice very low. 'I rather like it,' he added, and there was a smile at the back of his tone.

Anna felt power ebb away from her, even as she felt it building up in him, exuding from him. There was power in the very gentleness with which his fingers came up to clasp her chin and turn her face towards his;

power in the way the other arm tightened about her shoulders as his other hand slowly, rhythmically stroked her upper arm. And yet, even in the very act of surrendering her own power, she felt that it was replacing itself with a new strength: a quality which was fresh and young and vigorous, filling her with possibilities so that she was more potent, more female, more human than ever before.

'Neil . . .' She only just had time to murmur his name—and already it was too late. The bond was there between them, had been there all along, she knew that as well as he did. It had needed only this simple physical enactment, as inevitable as night following day. When their lips touched, she welcomed the shudder of electricity which shook her, instead of rejecting it as she always had before, on the few occasions she had even allowed anyone to get this far. Rather than enduring the intimate contact for as long as she could bear it, she invited it, relished it. Everything in her took on a new shape and a new form, rising to meet the new feeling.

At first his kiss was the softest, most experimental flutter she had ever encountered. Then, as her mouth gradually melted beneath his, giving itself up to his, he grew into a different creature—something alien, hard, demanding. Now her body discovered a life of its own. Instead of breaking away in disgust at the command of her mind, it leaped into wanton flames, astonishing the part of her brain which remained detached, watching the responses of the rest of her with horrified disapproval. Over the next few minutes even that cold part of her mind blurred, becoming indistinct and finally fading away into a pathetic, meaningless little nagging whine a long way off.

Her mouth, her hands, her whole body followed instincts and desires that were independent and untaught, allowing Neil's mouth and hands to explore them, invade them, possess them. She was shameless, mindless, nameless: an accumulation of female need for the first time in twenty-nine circumspect years. The effect was shattering—devastating—an explosion in her senses.

It was Neil who pulled away at last to gaze down at her, his blue eyes profoundly tender and yet glittering strangely like broken glass. 'Anna . . .' Whispered at such a moment, her name took on a whole new meaning. He kissed her again, lingeringly; then, reluctantly, he took charge of himself, drawing back, both her hands still clasped in his.

The power was still firm on his side, and Anna was unable to meet his intense gaze. Knowing her lips were still trembling and glistening from the touch of his, she stared down into her lap, deeply flushed, already aware of pangs of regret as her mind creaked back into action again.

'Anna,' he said again, softly, bending his head to try and look into her hidden face, 'we both knew what we were generating between us—didn't we? All that: it only swells and grows, the longer you leave it unresolved.' Waiting to see whether she would answer, he tightened his grip on her hands; but she remained withdrawn, shocked, head bowed, dark lashes lowered to veil her from him. 'Believe me, Anna, I didn't expect it to happen—not here, now, like this. Not yet.' There was a ring of truth in the words, and she was tempted to believe them. In any case, her mind taunted, what did it matter whether he'd intended it to happen or not? Either way, it had indisputably, irrevocably happened.

Still voiceless, she shook her bent head. Then he leaned closer and his tone became more urgent. 'I'm sorry—Anna? Don't be angry; not with me or yourself. We both knew it was there,' he said again, 'at least it's in the open now.' He was gathering confidence, returning to normal. 'It needn't change anything, surely? You can still take Chris's case, can't you?'

She raised her head at that, finally looking him straight in the eye, amazement overcoming embarrassment. 'Of course it changes things, Neil.' Her voice was no more than a mutter, unsteady, but her words were clear and positive. 'How could I go on with your case after—after this?' Her gaze dropped again as she reddened painfully. 'It was irregular enough, accepting your invitation to lunch, but now . . .'

'Anna!' He dropped her hands to take her by the shoulders, shaking her gently. 'Don't be a little fool. What's a kiss between friends? We're two mature people, aren't we? Surely we can take a thing like this in our stride? We're not kids. You're the ultimate professional.' It was, she knew, almost a sneer, hitting her where it hurt most. 'Don't tell me you're going to give up on Chris just because you and I fancy each other?' he accused caustically.

She winced at the expression, which seemed a long way from how she felt about him. *Fancy each other?* That implied nothing but a basic animal attraction—sexual stimulation—and for her there was a whole lot more to it than that. Apparently, for him, there wasn't. The conflicts this case aroused were all in her, then; all on her side.

His taunt had gone straight to its mark, scraping her raw nerves. But surprisingly, it hardened Anna's resolution in an unexpected direction. Instead of going under and backing out further, she faced up to his challenge with a renewed defiance. If he was that impervious to her, as a person, then so could she be to him.

'All right, Neil. I won't give up on Chris—if you won't. If I go on with the case, you've got to come back on it, too!' Her eyes blazed with new-found determination. She was surprising herself almost as much as she surprised him.

His face became hard, wry with scepticism. 'You mean after this you'd still be willing to have *me* at the sessions?'

'Why not? We still need you there as much as ever; or rather Christopher does,' she reminded him pointedly. 'You said it yourself, it's been there between us all along.' Boldly, confidently, she turned his words neatly round to work for her. 'Christopher will never know this happened—so what's the difference?'

Neil's hands left her shoulders and he moved away from her, staring at her as if seeing her for the first time. Then he stood up, thrusting his hands into his pockets, and shaking his head. 'Wow! I said you were an unpredictable lady, and I'll say it again! I've got to hand it to you, Anna: you're nothing if not single-minded.' For a long minute they contemplated each other—she from the sofa, he standing in front of her, neither of them flinching. Then Neil shook his head again, his features tightening into a frown, a tiny muscle clearly twitching in his cheek. 'I can't do it, flower. Even less so, now, after this. I'm sorry.'

She went on staring up at him, her expression poised and deeply thoughtful. Then, in a sudden movement, she stood up, walked sedately away from him, picked up her bag from the floor, ran an automatic hand over her hair to tidy it. 'Okay, Neil, if you haven't got the guts. I agreed to meet you today in the hope that you'd change your mind—for your brother's sake, not mine. It seems I'm into a losing battle. If you're not up to it, I haven't got the time to waste. I'll do the best I can without you.'

She was gathering the power back into herself, welcoming it like a long-lost friend. At the door she turned to look at him again. He was still standing by the sofa, his face inscrutable and even hostile as he watched her. He made no attempt to speak or justify himself. It was as if they'd discovered a mutual language and then, equally instantly, forgotten it.

'Please take me back to the Unit now, Neil,' Anna said quietly. 'I don't want to keep my three o'clock client waiting.'

CHAPTER SIX

THE drive back was accomplished at record speed, in an atmosphere of strained silence. Anna found herself acutely, agonisingly aware of every breath Neil took, every glance from the sharp blue eyes into the driving mirror, every movement of the competent hands on gear lever or steering wheel. It was as if his body had become more real to her than her own. If only his thoughts and feelings were equally vivid!

Turning her head away from him to gaze out of her window, she stifled a small sigh. Neil, intent on whisking her through the traffic to arrive in time for her three o'clock appointment, appeared not to notice. In fact he seemed lost in his own contemplations; perhaps already far away from Anna, and perhaps not. She had no way of knowing, and he certainly wasn't telling her.

She was unfastening her seatbelt and reaching for the door handle before the car had even purred to a halt. Then she was standing on safe familiar ground—the pavement outside the clinic—throwing a quick 'thanks for the lunch' in his general direction, slamming the door and pivoting round on her heel without giving him the chance to reply. Seconds later she had disappeared into the building, eyes fixed resolutely ahead. Neil sat with hands resting lightly on the wheel, staring after her for a minute or so; then he shrugged slightly, signalled right and pulled the Rover out into the road.

At Thursday's session, Anna watched Christopher closely for signs of change. Did he know she'd been to his house? And if so, would it make any difference? Would he resent her intrusion into his domestic domain, or might it open up new channels of communication between them? This whole situation was an unknown quantity to Anna, and filled her with apprehension, as all unknown quantities did.

At first, Christopher was his usual impassive self, saying little and imparting nothing helpful even when he did. But gradually Anna's doubts were reinforced: he did know she'd been to his home, she was sure of it—and he was not pleased. She never mentioned the subject, and neither did Christopher; but he became steadily more silent and guarded than ever until he was more or less back to his original sullen mask. Anna began to give way to pangs of a rare and unprofessional despair.

It was probably their most difficult session yet, with both of them skirting round the central issue, Christopher obstructive and surly, Anna hesitant and tense. Afterwards, knocked out by nervous exhaustion, it was all she could do to plod through Friday and then the weekend. For once in her life she had no energy left even for a therapeutic burst of cooking, and Jonathan was surprised and gratified to find her joining him on Saturday evening in front of his television set, staring her way through programmes she would normally have scorned, glad of his cheerfully undemanding company.

By Monday she had made up her mind to confront Christopher with the facts—or rather the simple fact that she'd visited his house, met his housekeeper and had a quick business lunch with Neil; no need to delve any deeper than that. Honesty was the only policy here, otherwise it was clear to her that they were going to remain totally static in the sessions, or perhaps even slide backwards. In any case, Anna reckoned, it might be a useful device in itself, telling him the truth: if he became openly angry with her for interfering, it could be just the trigger he needed in order to release some of that pent-up hostility.

Relaxed and composed in her armchair, she greeted him with her customary warmth and invited him to sit opposite her. Before she could take the plunge and air what was on both their minds, Christopher himself pre-empted her. Bolt upright in his chair, briefly abandoning his usual slouch, he faced her squarely and barked, 'Why didn't you tell me?'

Anna sat back, crossing one leg over the other. 'Tell you what, Chris?'

'You know what. That you came to my house.'

She regarded him thoughtfully. 'So you know about it, do you?'

'Yeah. Mrs R told me. Anyway . . .' he slumped, perhaps already regretting his direct attack, 'I saw you when you arrived. I heard Neil's car and I happened to look out of my window . . .'

'. . . and there I was.' Anna nodded sympathetically, picturing the scene and his reaction to it. 'And you wondered why I was there?' Christopher nodded gloomily. 'Why didn't you come down and find out for yourself?' Anna pressed.

Christopher grunted. 'I never come down in the daytime. Anyhow I didn't want to.' He pouted, like a petulant child. 'Why should I?'

'Why should you?' Anna agreed pleasantly. 'And didn't Neil tell you I was coming—or that I'd been, afterwards?' She tacked the question on airily, as if the answer wasn't really important.

'No.' Christopher frowned and brooded, his eyes troubled. Obviously this was what upset him most: his brother's secrecy. As he saw it, Anna belonged to both of them, in fact she was Christopher's property rather than Neil's. The idea of Neil inviting her to their home without consulting him, or even including him, had plunged him into a jealous paranoia. Anna could understand his feelings only too well—just as she could understand Neil's reasons for manipulating the whole dubious episode in the first place.

Christopher had hunched his lanky shoulders and withdrawn into himself. Anna had a vivid sensation that she was losing him, and had to fight down a most uncharacteristic panic. 'Did you actually ask Neil outright why I was there?'

Christopher went on staring morosely through the window, and Anna's heart sank still further. She must take a grip on the situation, win his trust again. She tried a new approach. 'What did Mrs R tell you?' she probed gently.

Reluctantly Christopher managed to collect a few words together. 'Nothing, till I asked her. Then she just said Neil had invited you to lunch, that's all.'

'That was all, Christopher,' Anna assured him earnestly—wishing to God it had been.

He glared at her sceptically, and she knew just how excluded he had felt. 'What did you talk about?' he mumbled.

'About your case, of course,' she told him with quiet candour. 'I went there for one reason: to try and persuade Neil to come back and join us here.'

Christopher's haunted gaze dropped to his knees. 'Well,' he muttered, 'it's a pity you didn't, then.'

This was dead on target, and Anna winced. 'Yes, it's a pity, Chris, but at least I had a try.' When he made no comment, she went on eagerly, 'I don't often agree to meet clients or their relatives outside here. When I agreed to meet Neil, I didn't know we'd be going to your house. It's a lovely house, by the way,' she added warmly, 'I like it a lot. Mrs R, too. We had some of her delicious soup, and I tried to talk Neil round, but he wouldn't change his mind.'

Anna waited now, gauging the boy's possible response to her honesty. He might go over the edge into the anger he needed to offload. More likely, he would slip back into his shell, because it was Neil he really wanted to express his feelings to, not Anna. As she feared, he opted for the latter, and from then on it was a waste of time. She squeezed nothing more out of him—not about the house, nor Mrs R, nor even Neil; and when she tried pushing him back to memories of old days long gone but not forgotten, he clammed up tighter than ever. That newly gained, hard-won mature co-operation had apparently vanished without trace.

Thursday's session was even worse, without any glimmer of light. When the last client had left at the end of the afternoon, Anna sat at her desk, head in hands, allowing the spiral of problems to churn round in her mind. Without Neil, this case was teetering on the brink of total disaster, but he had made his position crystal clear: he was adamant that he was not coming back.

For her part, Anna had absolutely no intention of crawling to a man like that any more—pulling out the stops, pleading, pressurising, even (perish the thought!) using feminine wiles to bring him round. That last-ditch tactic might work for some women, but not for her; she had principles and scruples. No, she'd done what she could: stated the case fairly and firmly, broken her own rules in meeting him privately, taken a risk in even going that far—and regretted it ever since. The experience had marked her deeply, in body as well as mind, so that neither of them seemed to get any peace: sleep eluded her at night, tranquillity during the day. She was a mess, a travesty of her real, organised, rational self; and all because of her involvement with one powerfully intransigent man.

Neil Tyrell: Anna hoped fervently that she never had to see him again. No, she didn't. She wanted him back at Christopher's sessions. Why not face the truth: she wanted him, period. Oh, it was all too ridiculously confusing!

The buzz of her internal telephone sliced into her grim reflections, and she lifted a weary hand to pick it up. 'Yes?'

'Anna? You still here?' Pam's breezy tones echoed down the line.

'So it would seem,' she replied sourly, lacking the will to disguise her mood.

'Ah—well, if you're still receiving, you've got a visitor.'

Something in Pam's voice alerted Anna so that she unwittingly sat up straighter and stared into the mouthpiece as if expecting to see her visitor's identity through it. 'Oh yes?' she countered warily. 'A bit late, isn't it?'

'I told him you'd be wanting to get off home soon, but he . . ' Pam cleared her throat, and Anna suddenly envisaged the intruder, leaning on the counter-top, keenly following every word, making private comment impossible. 'It seems very important, Anna,' Pam concluded carefully.

Anna sighed, loudly enough, she hoped, for the visitor to hear down the line. 'Who is it, Pam?'

She knew quite well what the answer would be. 'Mr Tyrell, senior,' Pam told her unnecessarily. 'He says it's urgent—about Christopher,' she added.

'I see.' It was almost as if her unruly contemplations had conjured the man up. As if she wasn't having enough trouble coping with the fact of his existence, now he had to materialise, like a ghost revived! Realising the possible implications of this visit, Anna's brain jerked into lightning action. She tried to ignore the fact that her body also went into powered overdrive at the prospect of seeing him again, and concentrated on how best to deal with the imminent confrontation.

Of course, she could send him packing without seeing him. One part of her had a strong urge to do just that. But nothing would be achieved that way; and in any case, he might have something important to say. Perhaps he'd changed his mind about coming to the sessions: she couldn't risk losing him if he had. No, she must see him. Then again, she had her own feelings to consider: the anarchy he produced in her careful order. Perhaps it would be best to send him away . . .

Inevitably, the combined calls of duty and curiosity proved more compelling than emotional self-preservation. 'Okay then, Pam,' she said, 'send him along, please.'

'Right.' The line clicked and Anna slowly replaced her receiver. Almost at once her door resounded to a short sharp knock, then burst open before she had time to respond.

Neil seemed to fill the doorway, his gaze instantly locked with hers. Pulling the door shut behind him, he strode into the room to confront her across the desk. Involuntarily she stood up, pushing back her chair, to face him nearer his own level.

'Hallo again, Anna.' His tone was misleadingly bland, businesslike, but Anna knew this was no social call. He would never deliberately put himself on to her territory again unless it was vital.

'Good afternoon, Neil.' Her own voice emerged cool and contained. 'I didn't expect to see you here.'

'I didn't expect to be here,' he retorted immediately, his tone hardening. Then, making a clear effort to be amiable, he glanced towards the telephone and declared, 'I dislike disembodied voices, but I had to talk to you. I apologise for barging in without an appointment,' he added sardonically, 'but it was urgent, and I do prefer to communicate direct, in the flesh, as you recall.'

In the flesh: his calculated use of the phrase goaded Anna into unwelcome recollections, taunted her wayward body into alarming flutterings; but she kept her surface poise intact. 'Why, is something wrong?'

'Yes, something is.' Catching her flash of concern, he softened slightly. 'Not seriously; no dire emergency, don't worry. But enough of a crisis to bring me here to see you, Anna. I know you were about to go home, but I wanted to catch you when you wouldn't be busy with grateful customers. It won't take very long.'

She studied him for a moment; then she nodded and sat down, motioning to him to do the same. He drew up the other upright chair, planted himself on it and leaned one elbow on the desk top opposite her. Unthinkingly he stretched out a long leg so that it came into brief contact with hers under the desk. Anna recoiled at once like a person stung, tucking both feet well back beneath her own chair, safely out of his range—and wishing this flimsy Government issue furniture was twice as wide and three times as solid. Then she sat back and folded her arms, still scanning his face. 'Well?' she demanded, in the tone of one who has other preoccupations. 'It's about Christopher, I take it?'

Neil was patently unmoved by this show of hard-headed efficiency, and returned her scrutiny, lazy blue eyes gleaming with innuendo. 'What else would you and I have to discuss, Anna?' Then he became intense, leaning towards her over the desk. 'Look, these sessions—you and Chris—it's not going well, is it?'

'No.' There seemed little point in denying it.

'I thought so.' Neil looked depressed. 'He's gone right back to how he used to be, skulking in his den, refusing to come down to meals, not a word for anyone—not even Mrs R, and she's really upset. At least he was being quite decent to her, before...' He broke off, shaking his head and frowning.

'Before I came to lunch?' Anna suggested sweetly, not making it any easier for him.

Neil glanced at her, then shrugged. 'Maybe,' he agreed non-committally. 'I left it a few days before I contacted you, because I thought he might have to get worse before he could get better; but today I couldn't risk leaving it any longer.'

'Why?' In spite of herself, Anna gave way to a note of anxiety. 'What's the matter? Isn't he home yet?'

'Oh, he's home all right. But he was later than usual, and looked ghastly—there was this hard, harsh look in his eye, worse than the usual gloom somehow... it was almost—I don't know,' he searched for the word, 'manic. He wouldn't say where he'd been on the way home, and he shouted at Mrs R and swore at me, then locked himself away. She was quite scared so I said I'd come straight round here.'

Anna's own mood was not exactly lightened by this piece of news. 'Well, I don't know what you expect me to do about it, Neil. We'd better make sure he's escorted here and back in future, I suppose, as he used to be.' She heaved a deep sigh. 'I did warn you,' she reminded him tautly, 'that without your active support things might easily deteriorate. The small progress we all noticed was entirely due to your presence and participation.'

'So it's been getting worse since I stopped coming?'

'Of course. Surely you don't need me to tell you that?' She was brusque, implicitly condemning him for his stubborn refusal to give way.

Neil's eyes narrowed: he resented criticism. 'Naturally

I could tell, but I wanted your official confirmation. Chris has been like a different bloke this last week. That's why I'm here,' he admitted irritably.

Anna spread both hands in a gesture of stoic resignation. 'There you are, then. The worst has happened, just as I was afraid it would if you backed out.'

Suddenly Neil was aggressive, running agitated fingers through his blond mane. 'But is it really that simple, Anna? Why should I take your word for it? After all, your professional judgment is at stake now, so how do I know you're not making him like this on purpose, to get back at me for my refusal to keep on coming?'

'What?' The accusation was so breathtakingly unfair that Anna's reaction emerged as a shriek, her mouth falling open in sheer astonishment. 'Are you implying what you seem to be implying, Neil?'

'Well,' he sneered, 'it's hard for a mere layman like me to credit that such a skilled practitioner as yourself, *Dr* Coleman, could allow a case to degenerate so far, so fast . . .'

'I don't believe this!' It was Anna's turn to lean across the desk, confusion and anger at this unwarranted attack surging through her in equal proportions. 'Let me get it right. You're suggesting that I could be continuing with the progress we were making earlier, but that I choose not to because I'm slightly miffed by your desertion from the case?'

'Something like that.' Neil thrust his hands into his pockets, eyeing her guardedly, his cool blue gaze taking in her heightened colour, the fire in her eyes.

'Neil . . .' Her voice shaking, caught completely off balance, Anna had to select each word with care. 'I've never heard of anything so ludicrous. The idea that I might sacrifice a client's wellbeing to some private whim—some foolish piece of personal pride—just to get even with you for opting out . . .!' For once, words failed her, and she could only stare at him, hurt and outraged.

But Neil was unrepentant, pushing his advantage. 'There may be other reasons why you'd want to get back at me,' he grated. 'My leaving the case might not be more important than Chris's progress—but my personal effect on you might be.'

It was a *tour de force*, well below the belt, and he knew it. Anna's eyes and mouth opened even wider as she groped for an answer, but no sound came out, no words formed themselves. The cheek, the sheer unadulterated *nerve* of such a suggestion . . . and yet the deadly aim of the second part of it, full on target! For a piece of irrational reason, or illogical logic, it couldn't be beaten.

He continued to stare at her impassively, and she fought to regain a little of the composure he had so successfully shattered, ever since he had walked into her life, when nothing and no one had ever managed to before. At last she located her voice, and a few clipped, well-chosen words. 'Neil, you're—you're sadly misguided if you really think anyone in my trade could operate at that level. I don't—I can't deny I was put out by what happened between us the other day. I wasn't even expecting to find myself in your home, let alone . . .' For the first time she lost her nerve.

Neil seized his chance. 'Let alone in my arms.'

Anna forced her eyes to meet his. All this was difficult enough, but frankness was probably the only way through it now. 'Quite,' she murmured. Then she found a reserve of strength, along with the honesty, and heard herself adding, 'I can't pretend I wasn't personally affected by what happened, Neil. You knew I was. But I'd never—*never*—let a thing like that interfere with the way I approach a case.' The truth of that statement lent her emphasis.

Neil's response was equally vehement, and totally unexpected, throwing her off balance all over again. 'No, Anna, you wouldn't.' Suddenly he was relaxing, leaning back, linking his fingers behind his head as he gazed reflectively at her, his eyes softening even as she watched—mesmerised, as always, by his every mood shift. 'I'm sorry, flower. I don't know what gremlin got into me and came out with that. I think I'm more worried about Chris than I realised.'

His warm smile went even deeper, cut even sharper in Anna than the arrogant belligerence had done. Was there no escape from the man's impact? 'It's okay, Neil, I understand,' she muttered, shyly returning the smile. Then she looked him full in the face and reminded him solemnly, 'Don't forget you're dealing with an expert in the subject of motivations.'

'How could I forget?' Neil stood up and walked to the window to stare out, just as he used to do at the end of an exhausting session. It felt similar, too, Anna found herself reflecting: that sense of drained relief. The brief exchange just ended—his explosion and subsequent humility, her admission of uncertainty after their physical encounter—had opened up a new dimension; an intimacy. Even as it terrified her, Anna welcomed it. He swung round now to face her, leaning on the wall by the window. 'Please accept my apology?'

Anna remained sitting calmly at her desk. For a few seconds they surveyed each other, a truce restored again. Then she replied, 'You know I'd always do my best for Chris, Neil, whether you were there or not. I said I'd keep on with the case after—after what happened the other day; and I will.'

'Even without my help.' Neil became self-mocking. 'You're twice the person I am, Anna.'

'Not at all,' she denied instantly. 'It takes plenty of character to look into yourself and apologise, as you've just done. I might have strengths,' she declared roundly, 'but I have my weaknesses, too.' *Only too obviously*, her mind added boringly.

It was as if Neil had read her thoughts. Suddenly he was grinning wickedly at her, causing a worse paralysis than ever. 'I suspect we might disagree over what you think of as your weaknesses,' he mused. They both knew he was absolutely right. 'If you were to ask me,' he went on, transferring his thoughtful gaze to the ceiling, 'I'd say they were some of your strongest assets.

Warm, human, responsive, instinctive, uncompli-
cated...' Then he was looking at her again, and the
grin had become a smile of genuine affection.

Swamped, as usual, with ambivalent feelings, Anna
was about to call the whole interview to order before it
got quite out of hand, when Neil took over the job for
her. He glanced at his watch and crossed the room to sit
opposite her again. 'This is all taking too long. We
haven't got anywhere yet. I came to say something, and
I've hardly started.' He was impatient with himself now.

Anna's dark brows lifted in surprise. Despite her
trained insight, he was an enigma to her. What on earth
was he about to come out with now? 'I can't tell you
any more about Chris's case,' she began hesitantly. 'As
you assumed, it's not going well, in fact we seem to be
moving backwards. But if you won't rethink your
position I can only keep trying. One day I expect I'll
spark off the necessary...'

'Shut up, Anna,' he cut in bluntly. 'Please,' he added,
his eyes gleaming at her incredulous stare. 'I came to
put a new proposition to you. It seems I had some other
garbage to get out of my system first,' he observed
drily.

'A new proposition?' she echoed dubiously, tightening
her guard against whatever he might decide to throw at
her next. 'What kind of bargain is it this time?'

His smile was rueful. 'I suppose that's a nicer word
than blackmail, and no less than I deserve.' He placed
both hands on the desk top, palms down. 'You
remember when you asked me about my next film and I
said I wanted to consult you about it?'

'Yes.' She nodded, recalling the occasion only too
clearly.

'Thought you might have let it slip your memory, in
view of immediate developments,' he teased, his tone
low and gently insinuating.

The colour rose in Anna's face and neck as if he had
pressed a switch, but she contrived to keep her voice
reasonably steady as she retaliated, 'I hope my brain
isn't as addled as all that.'

'Never let it be said,' he acknowledged gravely. 'Anyone less scatterbrained I have yet to meet. Anyway,' he continued briskly, 'I've got this great notion for my next project; and you could be a real help.'

'Oh yes?' Only a shrewd observer, such as Neil, could have guessed that Anna was burning with curiosity, laced with apprehension.

'Yes. What do you think about a programme dealing with your trade: a documentary on Child Psychology? Perhaps featuring a Unit like this, the way it runs, what you hope to achieve, your methods, the history of the profession and its antecedents . . .' He was lit up now, carried on a wave of creative inspiration. 'It would be just up my street. The human touch, but investigative, exploratory. I know I'd do it well, if I had the right support and advice,' he informed her confidently.

'I'm sure you would.' Even as she responded to his warmth, Anna had to admire his self-possession, that clear awareness of his own mastery when it came to his chosen vocation. He loved it, just as she loved hers. Altogether, the two of them had a lot in common, apart from that undeniable, uncomfortable sexual magnetism. Chemistry was one thing. He'd as good as confessed to it himself. But as far as her feelings were concerned, it went deeper than that. She not only respected and responded to him: she liked him. A far more exciting, far more fearsome prospect.

'So what do you think?' he nudged, as she seemed lost in contemplation.

'Not a bad idea.' Actually she thought it was a fine idea, but she was not in the habit of polishing up already inflated male egos.

'So would you help me, Anna, if I decided to follow it up?' He was eager now, and very persuasive. 'There'd be no problem with financial backing. I've done several things for an independent company who seem keen on the proposal. But I'd need contacts, facilities . . . talking heads, experts . . . you know the sort of thing, presumably, even if you don't waste your time watching the old goggle-box?' He shot her a wry glance.

'Of course I do! I haven't been totally protected from it all my life!' She glared at him. 'As a matter of fact I watch a neighbour's set quite often, when I'm in the mood. I've seen plenty of documentaries. I know exactly what you mean.'

'Mine,' he informed her solemnly, 'are generally reckoned to be accurate, intelligible and consistent. Which is more than you can say for some directors.'

'Brilliant, and modest with it.' She grinned; then she looked at him shrewdly. 'Did you have this idea when Chris started coming here, Neil?'

'Not at first. You know how prejudiced, not to say pig-ignorant, I was about the whole scene a year ago,' he confessed disarmingly. 'But when I saw how much good you were doing—how we really seemed to be getting somewhere . . .'

In spite of his candour, Anna couldn't resist a sardonic dig. 'So, even though you refuse to involve yourself any more, you still expect me to help you in your study of our aims and methods? That hardly seems—what was your word?—consistent,' she pointed out.

'I rather thought you might say something like that, and I don't blame you.' He chuckled disconcertingly.

'Sorry to be so predictable,' Anna retorted tartly. 'So you've got your answer all worked out?'

'Right. And you, wise lady as you are, don't need me to tell you what it is.'

Anna deliberated briefly; then she raised her eyes to his. 'Could it be that if I'll agree to help you, you'll agree to come back on the case?' she said slowly.

'Got it in one.' Without warning his hand snaked across the desk top to cover one of hers. 'Go on, Anna, say you'll do it. With your knowledge and my flair, we could come up with something really special.'

Anna's energy was completely absorbed at that moment, dealing with the electric current which pulsed through her at the touch of his skin, then in wondering whether he was ever going to stop ambushing her with new and tougher challenges. Eventually she calmed herself sufficiently to withdraw her hand from his, lift her head and look at him. 'I don't know, Neil. I'd rather you came back because you wanted to, not because you want something from me,' she told him quietly.

'Perhaps I do really want to come back, and this is my way of saying so,' he suggested gruffly.

Anna wondered which of them was the true psychologist. 'Anyway,' she prevaricated, 'I'm not sure I should take part in anything like that while I'm even remotely connected with Chris's case. It wouldn't be at all . . .'

'But do you *like* the idea? Would you do it, if everything else was equal?'

Anna was plunged into internal upheaval at the direct demand. On the one hand, acceptance would mean prolonged and deepened social contact between them, and that was fraught with risks and unknown factors. On the other, she wanted him back on the case, not to mention in her life, on almost any terms.

She opted for cautious noncommitment. 'I need time to think it over. I must discuss it with my colleagues here, for a start. They'd need to be involved, too.'

'The more the merrier,' Neil chanted, at once. 'I don't do things by halves, Anna.' The simple statement seemed multi-layered with implications. 'When I explore a subject, it's well and truly explored. Or, where necessary, exposed. Just like you,' he added airily, 'with people!'

She ignored the personal analogy, fighting to keep the thing on an objective footing. 'All the more reason why you should be nowhere near the arena at an emotional level before you start,' she pointed out firmly. Then she drew in a deep breath. 'If you'll come back to our sessions for a while, and see how it goes, then I might—*might*—think about taking part in your film. But not until there's more light at the end of Christopher's tunnel,' she emphasised.

Neil eyed her with grudging respect, tinged with amusement. 'I've got to hand it to you, Anna; you've got nerve. So, I'm to move back into your camp without even knowing for sure whether you'll finally agree to make your gracious services available?'

'That's a fair summary, yes.' Anna had regained her equilibrium now, and felt distinctly relieved.

'Hmmm.' Neil sat back and thought it over. 'I'll admit I was hoping for a more positive commitment than that. But I suppose I'm not in a position to argue.'

'No,' Anna said.

'Okay.' He was a man of decision and action. 'I'll rejoin the sessions, starting Monday. How's that?'

Just like that! After all the heart-searching and the jockeying for position! And now that she had achieved it, Anna's sense of triumph was diluted with at least an equal part of gut-wrenching apprehension. Why was nothing straightforward any more? 'Only because I've said I might agree to help with your project?' she hedged.

But Neil was ready for her. 'Because I want to help Chris. Believe it or not, Anna, he is my main concern. I'd have returned to the fold, sooner or later, once I was brave enough to face you there again.' His sincerity set her off balance yet again, and she sighed wearily, suddenly acutely tired.

'I wish you could have made it sooner, rather than later,' she snapped.

'I did have my reasons,' he shot back.

Anna opened her mouth to make a sharp retort, then closed it again. She needed peace and quiet to reflect on all this. Plenty of time to follow this one through later, when she held the reins again, when she had him pinned down in a session. But now she really was exhausted, and it was getting late. Yawning and stretching, she looked at the clock on the wall. Ten past six! Pam would be wondering what was going on, if she was still around; and if she'd gone home, Daniel must be still here or he'd have let her know he was leaving her to lock the premises up . . .

She turned back to Neil, ready to conclude the interview. But his chair was empty. He was already on his feet, walking round to penetrate that secure haven on her side of the desk. Then he was grabbing her hands and pulling her up to stand beside him, grasping her by the shoulders, drawing her shocked and unresisting body closer, closer to the potent magnet of his.

'I don't care whose patch we're on, Anna,' he was muttering hoarsely in her ear, 'it doesn't seem important any more. Oh, I came here to say all that. To talk about Chris, ask for your services, offer mine, I don't know ... but most of all, I came here because I had to see you again. To do this again,' he murmured, burying his face in her warm neck, his lips scorching a trail over her ear and the curve of her soft cheek.

And then he was doing it again, kissing her for a very long time, with a depth and a sensuality, a power and a promise which left her reeling: every cell alight, every thought a meaningless jumble of jargon. And she was returning the kiss with all that instinctive desire, clutching at his physical strength as if she would crumble into a spineless, formless heap without its support.

Anna's sanctum, that shrine to carefully organised human interaction, had never before witnessed a scene of quite such intense communication. Anna was much too far gone, too busy responding, to stop and remember where they were. But before the unconventional moment of therapy could run away with itself, reality intruded in the form of a buzzing desk telephone. Summoned back to sanity, she tried to break away, one hand groping towards the strident interruption, the other fluttering uselessly against Neil's chest. He released her and stepped back, but he took hold of both hands so that she could not pick up the receiver. The bell shrilled again, tearing Anna up like a symbol of all her inner conflicts.

'Neil! I'll have to answer it! They'll wonder what the hell ...'

His smile was tender and ironic all at once, melting its way through her few remaining defences. 'I'm going now. When I've gone, you can answer it. I must get back anyway; I promised Mrs R I wouldn't be long.' Drawing her into his arms again, he bent to kiss her lightly on the eyes, nose and mouth. Then he turned to walk to the door. The 'phone rang again. Anna gazed at it, then at him, wrenched by indecision. She moved towards it, but she let it go on ringing.

Reaching the door he smiled round at her, calm and composed. 'See you Monday when I report for duty. And, Anna,' he paused, fingers resting on the handle, 'when you've got me in your clutches again—be gentle with me, won't you?'

Then he was gone, and for a few seconds she stared at the closed door, attempting to pour cold streams of reason on to the flames that still flickered, until they were reduced to smouldering embers: the hottest part of the fire, left at the end.

Neil's parting quip had been more than half in earnest. At one level, he was putting himself willingly into her hands. At another, much deeper one, he had only just demonstrated how easily, how totally, how devastatingly he could take the power into his. It was like being on a seesaw, perfectly poised, rocking either way: but in the end, she knew well enough, Neil would weigh the heavier.

With a last fruitless effort at soothing her still pulsating senses, she reached for the telephone just as it buzzed for the fourth time.

CHAPTER SEVEN

NEIL'S return to the case worked miracles on a scale even Anna had hardly foreseen. Those painful sessions, when she and Christopher had sparred politely as she made futile attempts to dig real responses out of him, were instantly transformed into exciting hours of lively communication. Neil had obviously decided to bring along a renewed vigour, a reinforced sense of purpose, and Christopher responded at once, picking up the progress he had been making earlier and continuing with it as if it had never been broken. Anna heaved a metaphorical sigh of relief.

Twice a week without fail, for nine weeks, Neil threw his indomitable spiritual energy into the sessions, and Anna knew he was making this his top priority for the moment. In the light of his brother's unwavering concentration, Christopher emerged from his shell, slowly at first but then with increasing momentum, expanding steadily in confidence and warmth before their eyes. Keeping her tight rein on proceedings, directing their exchanges from her corner, Anna allowed herself to admit to a ripening involvement with them both, and especially a deepening respect for Neil as each new stage of Christopher's growth passed smoothly by. But it was vital that she should maintain a strictly professional approach if they were to succeed in their joint enterprise, stifling any personal feelings until it was concluded. Neil showed his own understanding of this, controlling his own attitude to her at a brisk, undemanding level with only the occasional penetrating glance or comment to disturb the surface calm. Wrapping himself up in developments concerning Christopher, he turned to Anna as the objective third party, the agent acting between them.

Without her skill and influence, of course, none of

these developments could have taken place, and they knew that as well as she did. During the intervening days, while she dealt with other clients, or embarked on a batch of baking, or sat down to write some notes, she often found herself pausing to reflect on the Tyrell case. It was with her all the time; she had never been so acutely conscious of any case blossoming into a mutual opening-up. Neil, although officially only going through all this for Christopher's benefit, was learning plenty about himself. As for Anna—well, layers were unfolding inside her which she suspected had no place in her life, least of all in her consulting room, with every hour she witnessed him in forceful action.

Throughout this time Anna encouraged them to explore every aspect of their lives together since Christopher's birth—except one. She steered them carefully away from the single delicate topic which had precipitated such a dramatic rejection in Neil before: the exact nature of their parents' final tragic accident. Chris had now shed many tears over their loss, Anna had alluded to it, even Neil had skirted round it, but the full details were never spelled out again. The very word, 'drowning', was studiously avoided as if by common consent.

Yet it was always there in the background, a shadow waiting to encroach, a cloud forming on the horizon, and Anna knew it would have to be cleared out of the way before they could quite claim to be finished. As far as Christopher was concerned, they had achieved as much as anyone could have hoped. Freed from hidden deposits of jealousy, fear and grief, he was a different boy, a rediscovered person. Glowing reports from the social workers, from Mrs R and from Neil himself confirmed this, even if it had not been obvious just from talking to him. Anna was preparing her own report on him now, in which she would officially state that in her opinion his emotional and psychological problems had been severe but were now substantially behind him, and that he should be dealt with leniently by the court, put on probation but allowed to get on with his life.

No, this particular block was really Neil's, however much he preferred to deny or ignore it, and Anna was determined not to let the case close without helping him to break through it. Biding her time, leaving it to one side, she waited for the right moment to attack it again. Finally, during the Monday session of what was to be their last week, she took the plunge and pushed them deliberately back into those stormy waters.

Neil had just made a teasing reference to the fact that it had taken Christopher a long time to learn to swim. 'I can remember you kicking and screaming at the pool,' he recalled, grinning affectionately at his brother, 'while Father supported you from underneath and Mother shouted instructions. We thought you'd never stay afloat.'

Christopher's grin was equally direct. 'Just because you could swim from the day you were born!' he grumbled. 'Anyway,' he declared with spirit, 'I can beat you at table tennis.'

'Only because I let you,' Neil retorted firmly.

Anna interrupted this light-hearted banter with a mild enquiry. 'So how old were you when you did manage to stay afloat?'

Christopher looked vague. 'I don't know—about six, I s'pose?'

Anna smiled at him. 'That doesn't seem old to me. I can only just swim now.'

'Yes, but Neil was a real water baby,' Christopher explained, without rancour. 'He could swim almost before he could walk—or so I was always told.' He shot a sceptical glance at his brother.

'Oh, I could, I could,' Neil assured them airily. 'I was one of those precocious kids. An early devotee of skin-diving, water-skiing, rock-climbing, pot-holing . . . not to mention more intellectual pursuits: chess, Scrabble, canasta . . .'

Christopher giggled, but Anna had recognised the chance she had been looking out for and decided to seize it. 'What about your parents—were they keen swimmers?'

There was a short tense silence. Then Neil said, as if unwillingly, 'They had to be, really, or they wouldn't have made very good sailors.'

'Not all sailors can swim,' pointed out Christopher logically.

'True enough, but most can. And they certainly could,' Neil stated, his tone curiously deadpan but emitting clear warning signals to Anna to stay off the subject.

Naturally this only hardened her resolve to expose it. 'I was only wondering whether their lives might have been saved if they'd have been stronger swimmers.' She looked boldly, even defiantly, from one to the other, encountering bleak hostility in Neil's face and surprised agitation in Christopher's, but she pressed on anyway. 'Or perhaps they weren't wearing lifebelts?' she suggested mildly.

'They always wore lifebelts.' It was Neil's turn to growl, and slump in his chair, expression withdrawn and body taut just as Christopher's had been weeks ago.

Christopher, in his new-found mature honesty, rounded on Anna to demand angrily, 'What did you have to go and say that for? Can't you see it's made him upset?' His glance at Neil was deeply compassionate, almost protective.

'Yes, I can see that, Chris,' she told him quietly. 'And that's exactly why I had to ask it.' There was something touching, even moving, about the boy's eagerness to defend his brother. At this minute it was the two of them pitted against her. Although she had engineered this confrontation intentionally, and had plenty of experience in such challenges, Anna found herself clenching up—heart racing, breathing shallow, palms sticky.

'We told you before,' Christopher reminded her reproachfully, as Neil remained silent but studied her through harshly resentful blue eyes, 'there was a freak storm. Even a strong swimmer couldn't have survived what it did to the boat. It was smashed up on some rocks under the water. The sea was all churned up.' Anna veiled her own sick anxiety as she watched him closely. He paled at the memory but he rose to the test, holding her gaze with his. 'I was only small but I can still remember those waves. You could see them from the window of our cottage. Even in the harbour they were huge; outside they must have been . . .' He shivered. 'I do still dream about them sometimes,' he admitted steadily.

Anna was torn between sheer pleasure at the change in this boy who had so recently been no more than a sullen, crumpled heap of depression, and concern for the man who was clearly so profoundly sensitive on this subject. 'It must have been awful for you, Chris— awful.' She was firm and gentle, genuinely appalled again at the image. 'But perhaps you were too young to understand what was really happening. Neil wasn't.' She turned to meet Neil's angry glare head-on, as serenely as possible. 'Will you tell me a bit more about it, Neil? Please?' Her tone was low, persuasive.

He squared his shoulders, making a clear effort to pull himself together. 'Why?' he barked—abrasive, aggressive. 'Why should I? Haven't you squeezed enough out of me, these past weeks, without extracting this last ounce?'

Anna winced, even in the full knowledge that his fury was aimed less at her than at himself. For some reason—and she was going to get to the bottom of it right now, if it killed her—he was nursing a gnawing secret connected with this incident. There was something more here than the inevitable trauma such a shock must cause. After all, he had been (as he had pointed out to her in no uncertain terms) a grown man at the time, and a far from weak one.

She drew a deep breath and faced him placidly. 'I don't intend to close this file, Neil,' she indicated the folder which lay shut, as usual, on her lap, 'without finding out the truth about this. You could say it was at the heart of the case.'

'You know the truth,' he flung back, his eyes accusing. 'I've told you.'

Before she could reply, Christopher was arresting their attention. 'But, Anna, I'm okay now, aren't I? We're here because of me, not Neil. Can't we just let it go? Do we have to think about it any more?'

Anna smiled at him and shook her dark head. 'I'm sorry, Chris, I'm afraid we do. You're fine now, yes, and that's great—and perhaps this isn't really your problem; but in a way any problem that's Neil's is yours, too. Don't you agree?'

He nodded doubtfully. 'Yeah, I s'pose so.'

'Well, he's been helping you with yours; now it's your turn to see him through one of his. All right?'

Put that way, Christopher could hardly refuse. 'Okay,' he agreed.

Neil had been absorbing this exchange with an air of dry irony. Now he folded his arms and cleared his throat significantly. 'I hate to interfere in this tender little scene,' he drawled, 'but don't I get some say in this? If it's *my* problem, shouldn't *I* be the first to know about it, and ask for help with it? It's too kind of you both to work for my welfare, but actually . . .'

'Neil.' Anna cut him off sharply before he could resort to still deeper sarcasm in self-defence. 'I am not signing this case off until you tell us—both of us— everything you remember about that day. Never mind whether it's for your sake, or Chris's, or just for mine. Let's just say I must set the record straight, tie up the ends, and this is one of them.'

Neil stared intensely into her eyes for several seconds, then seemed to relax, shrugging in wry resignation and crossing one long leg comfortably over the other. 'Fair enough, flower. You're the expert. You know best. The sooner we can tie up the ends, the better. If this is the last fence, I'm not one to refuse it.'

It was the first time in all these weeks that he had lapsed into the old belligerence, but at least he hadn't stormed out. 'It's the last fence, Neil,' Anna assured him softly.

Arms still tightly folded, he fixed his gaze on a point outside the window. 'Right.' His voice took on an automatic, droning quality as if he was trying to pretend the words came from somewhere else rather than within him. 'I believe I told you the parents were quite used to sailing their own ketch, but not my little dinghy.'

'Yes?' Anna encouraged as he hesitated. Christopher sat quietly, intent.

'On the whole they were fair-weather mariners. Preferred short pleasure trips, flat seas, anchoring somewhere nice and secluded for a swim and a picnic—you get the picture. Mother liked her creature comforts. She made a great first-mate in a holiday mood, but her idea of fun wasn't being thrown about in a tiny tub like mine.'

'So why did they go out in it that day?' Anna prompted when he paused again.

'That day,' Neil's tone was warming up, his face becoming tense and flushed, 'Father and I had been having an almighty row.'

This came as no great surprise to his listeners. One of the important facts to emerge during these weeks was that Neil and his father had not, on the face of it, enjoyed a smooth or easygoing relationship. In fact they had spent much of the time baiting each other. 'Probably too alike for our own good,' Neil had muttered when the topic had been aired on a previous occasion. 'He never seemed to approve of anything I did, even when I did it well. Especially when I did it well,' he had amended on a thoughtful note. 'After all, he was only in his mid-forties and still very athletic. In a way,' Neil had mused, half to himself, 'I think we were fighting over Mother. Very Freudian, no doubt,' he had added sardonically.

'They used to really bellow at each other,' Christopher had recalled, with his quick grin. 'Mother and I usually kept out of the way while the sparks flew.'

Anna was recycling all this in her mind now, but she pushed Neil on, loath to let him lose impetus when he'd finally got under way at last. 'Can you remember what it was about this time?'

Neil's face was haunted now, shadowed. 'Not really. The same old stupid rivalry, I suppose.' He frowned as he searched his memory for the truth. 'All I know is it turned into a ridiculous wrangle over our two yachts, with both of us behaving like contentious idiots. I remember saying you couldn't call it real sailing, in that fine thing with all its luxurious trappings and space-age equipment, even automatic pilot. If you wanted a true sense of achievement you had to be master of a small craft, pit yourself against the elements, preferably racing before a good head wind. Racing was my obsession at the time,' he broke off to inform them, his tone brittle. 'I've always been competitive,' he confessed, 'but if I got that from anyone, it was him,' he declared bluntly.

This was breaking new ground, and both Anna and Christopher were nodding sympathetically as they willed Neil to unburden himself once and for all. But he was apparently oblivious to them, or to anything else in the present as his eyes focused inside his mind for a clearer view of a past so long buried it had become obscure. 'I threw out a challenge. I remember saying it. God knows why . . .' His voice cracked but he regained control. 'I told him he was all mouth, had no idea what he was talking about, wouldn't know how to manage a small dinghy like mine even if he had to.' Neil closed his eyes tightly, as if against pain; then found the strength to open them and carry on. 'He shouted at me that I needn't think I had the advantage, just because I was over twenty years younger, and he could do anything I could. Next thing I knew, he was getting ready to go out, and Mother was saying she wasn't going to miss her day's sailing for anyone. Anyway, she always took his side.' A suppressed bitterness was mounting in his tone. 'They did everything together, those two.'

Some interesting flotsam was rising to the surface now. Anna held her breath, afraid he might dry up at this crucial point, but she had no need to worry. Neil was well into his stride and clearly had no intention of admitting defeat this time. 'They set off for the beach. I let them go; never said another word. I knew where they were going because you had to take the car to where the ketch was moored, but you could walk down to the bay where I left the dinghy.' So, he was implying, he could not hide behind innocence: he had been implicated from the start. 'It was a breezy day, but looked set fair. We watched through the window— didn't we, Chris?' He turned suddenly to his brother as if for confirmation.

'I seem to remember coming into the room after they'd left, and you were standing at the window, staring out,' Chris recalled slowly. 'You did seem sort of strange, but I didn't know why, and then—well, I must have forgotten about all that, after ... when ...' He faltered, but kept his head high and his tone firm.

Anna was proud of him. 'So what happened?' The rest was history, but she had to force Neil to describe it.

'You know what happened, Anna.' His eyes glittered with anger that was laced with appeal. 'Do I have to spell it out again?'

'Yes, you do,' she instructed simply.

He stiffened, but accepted her dictum, perhaps assuming it was for Christopher's sake as much as his own. 'We saw them cross the bay under motor power, then hoist sail and set off round the headland. Even as we stood there, these massive black jagged clouds crept across the sky, blotting out the sun.' He was shaken, all at once, by an involuntary shudder. Anna glanced at Christopher, but the boy was poised, his only concern apparently for Neil as he spurred himself on. 'That wind sharpened in the space of five minutes, I swear it, into a force nine gale. Just like that. We could hear it, and see it in the trees, and that sea built up into a good old lather ... but they'd gone, disappeared. There was nothing I could do, except perhaps warn the coast-guards; but that seemed silly when there was nothing, as far as I knew, to warn them about ...'

Anguish flooded his voice as he recaptured those desperate minutes. Christopher bit his lip, on the verge of sympathetic tears. 'Nothing I could do!' Neil repeated, as if intoning an agonised incantation which he had chanted hundreds of times, over the years, in his head or under his breath.

'Nothing anyone could do.' Anna leaned over to lay a hand on his arm, but he shook it off roughly and swung round to face her, his expression utterly grim. She saw a tear, the first ever, standing at the corner of one of his eyes, and her breath caught in her throat. She had brought him to the crunch at last.

'You see now—it was my fault! The whole thing was my fault!' he groaned. 'Goading him like that, then letting him go, and letting Mother go with him—I could have stopped them!' Neil covered his face with his hands, allowing his pent-up emotions free rein for once: shedding rare, cleansing tears, a man's tears, accompanied by violent sobs which convulsed his powerful body.

Anna knew he could still hear her, in spite of everything, and she spoke to him, because this was the time to speak. 'It was no more your fault than your father's,' she told him urgently. 'Probably less. He should have stopped to consider, especially before involving your mother. It was his responsibility. You've been blaming yourself for years, and your guilt has become a wall inside you, so that you could never show any feelings or let out any grief—or help Chris to let his out,' she added, compelling in her certainty. 'Listen to me, Neil. This is the end of all that. The wall's down, and the guilt's gone. You can't afford to blame yourself any more, for that day or for all those fights you had with your father, or for the accident. Especially for the accident—*it was an accident*,' she emphasised slowly. 'And now that you've told us all that, you'll be able to stop.'

Then she sat back because she knew she had said and done all she could for them both, and waited for the last link in the chain: Christopher's reaction. The boy

had been staring at his brother through blue eyes round
with consternation mingled with sudden comprehension.
As soon as Anna had finished speaking, he got up from
his chair and walked across to crouch beside the
hunched figure of Neil, heaving out the dregs of his
remorse. The boy's skinny arms crept about the man's
solid frame, clasping it close for the first time, perhaps,
in many years. Would Neil reject this physical gesture,
or accept it? At first there was no visible response at all;
but gradually, as Anna watched, blinking back her own
tears, the man's muscular arm firmly encircled the boy's
shoulders in silent overdue acknowledgement of a
lifetime's unspoken, undemonstrated love and
attachment.

Neil's sobs subsided as rapidly as they had started,
and Anna knew he would never need them again.
Christopher, on the other hand, had buried his face in
the safety of Neil's strong neck and was weeping—from
joy and release as much as shared sorrow. Calmly
accepting his brother's tears, Neil raised his fair head
proudly at last, looking over to where Anna always sat
at the third point in the triangle.

But her place was empty. She had slipped away a few
minutes earlier, leaving them to complete their
recognition scene in privacy together, and also seriously
afraid that if she stayed any longer she would give way
to a strong temptation to gather Neil into her arms and
comfort him, pour out all her own pent-up feelings, and
that would hardly have been suitable. No, she had
achieved what she had set out to achieve for the Tyrells.
The rest was up to them.

CHAPTER EIGHT

THURSDAY'S session had been officially designated the Tyrells' last, and for the next two days Anna was on edge. Would they turn up? Had Monday's climactic, cathartic scene proved too much for them, or would they see it through to the end?

After slipping from the room, she had left them to see themselves off, keeping a low profile in the staff room until Pam rang through to tell her they had gone, so she had no idea how they had looked or felt when they left. She knew she must contain her suspense, which lasted until the new cheerful Christopher appeared punctually at her door on Thursday. There was no sign of Neil.

Anna smiled in response to his friendly grin. 'Hallo, Chris! All alone?'

'We weren't sure if you wanted us both today, so I just came along to say goodbye.' He shuffled from one large foot to the other. 'And, you know, thanks, and all that.' The blue gaze—suddenly disconcertingly reminiscent of Neil's—dropped, and the youthful cheeks flushed as embarrassment temporarily overcame self-confidence. Shoving his hands into the pockets of his Harrington jacket, he flung his lanky frame into one of the waiting armchairs.

Anna steeled herself against a tremor that shot through her at the finality of his words. *Goodbye-and-thanks*: a conventional dismissal, a signing-off. For one crazily irrational moment she found herself wondering helplessly whether she would ever set eyes on either of them again. Then she admonished herself roundly: such partings were an occupational hazard of her job. She should never have allowed herself to become so involved in a case if she hadn't expected to suffer when it was successfully concluded. It was an object lesson which she must take to heart and

131

never forget, if her career was to go from strength to strength.

'I was hoping you'd come,' she assured him calmly. 'I wanted to talk to you once more before closing this lot.' She indicated the file in her lap. 'I could have done with another few words with Neil, too,' she added nonchalantly, 'but not to worry.'

Christopher had rapidly recovered his poise. 'Oh, he'll be along to fetch me. He said he'd look in at the end of the hour in case you wanted to say anything.'

Adopting her most matter-of-fact tone and de-meanour, Anna crossed one slim leg, clad in tan cotton dungarees, over the other. 'Good.' Then she smiled across at Christopher as she opened the file for one last time. 'Just a routine form he has to sign. I always say that every hour I spend in consultation generates another hour of paperwork.' She shook her head ruefully. 'Anyway, Chris, I've got a few well-chosen words to say to you, so perhaps it's not such a bad thing you're here on your own.'

'Yeah, that's what we thought,' Christopher agreed sagely, conjuring up such a vivid image of co-operative discussion and communication between the two brothers that Anna almost laughed aloud in a sudden burst of triumphant delight. Here was a success story, and no mistake: on one level, at least, she had achieved a genuine transformation.

Under her gentle encouragement Christopher chatted easily and openly about the way he saw his life now, as a result of these last few weeks: how he remembered his past, how he envisaged his future. His freedom from the severe depression which had gripped him was so recent, and perhaps fragile, it was too soon to be making concrete plans. But his attitude was positive and optimistic, and Anna felt proud of him. She knew instinctively that whatever he decided to do next, he was going to do it wholeheartedly. Even more important, he was going to do it without the false support of artificial stimulants, but with the true and renewed support of his elder brother.

After forty minutes Anna closed the file with a snap and sat back, her hazel eyes warm on his face. 'I'm going to miss your sessions, Chris.'

'Me, too,' He grinned, then studied the pattern on the carpet. A short, companionable silence was broken by the buzz of the telephone.

Anna crossed to her desk to answer it. 'Yes?'

'Mr Tyrell's arrived,' Pam's crisp voice informed her. 'Shall I send him through?'

'Please, Pam.' Replacing the receiver, Anna came round to lean on the front of her desk. 'Neil's here,' she told Christopher.

The boy uncurled himself from the chair and stretched. Anna reflected inconsequentially that he was going to be even taller than his brother, but probably never quite so striking. 'Shall I make myself scarce?' he suggested. 'I expect you two'll want to have a good moan about me behind my back.'

Anna pulled a face at him. 'Not a moan, no. The opposite if anything. But it might be a good idea if you waited in reception, yes. I might say things that would swell your head if you heard them.'

Christopher grinned again and made for the door. Then, as if recollecting something, he stopped, turned and came back. Solemnly he held out his right hand to her, flicking back a stray lock of dark-blond hair with his left. 'Thanks, Anna—for everything, you know. You've been . . .' He cleared his throat. 'Fantastic.'

Touched and surprised, Anna could only take the offered hand and shake it warmly. 'I won't say I was only doing my job, Chris.' *I've learned better than that, at least*, her mind added wryly. 'That sounds insulting. I don't often find cases as . . ' she searched for a word that would sound personal without being unprofessional, 'intriguing as yours,' she told him carefully. 'I'm really glad we made it through together—with Neil's help. Perhaps we'll meet again sometime, in easier circumstances.' Suddenly she sounded strangely wooden and formal, but the only real alternative was to give him a hug, and she knew that would be going to the other extreme.

'Maybe.' The single word was non-committal, but it was belied by Christopher's expression of hopeful affection. He dropped her hand as a sharp knock echoed through the room. ' 'Bye, then.' He walked briskly to the door, almost colliding with Neil as he opened it. 'See you later,' he muttered to his brother, and with a last quick wave in Anna's direction he was gone.

Neil shut the door firmly behind Christopher and then leaned back against it, allowing his penetrating gaze to sweep over her. He hooked both thumbs into the belt of his canvas jeans and bent one long leg up at the knee. 'Unless I'm much mistaken,' he declared sarcastically, 'that was a tear I saw trembling in baby brother's blue eye. Parting is such sweet sorrow?'

Anna stiffened instantly at his tone, her glance flying up to investigate his face. So, she had been right: he was regretting that display of honest emotion on Monday. He was most probably furious with her for perpetrating it; breakthrough it might have been but it had presented too deep a threat, after all, to his self-image.

His expression gave little away, the hard planes of it as unyielding as ever now that the two of them were alone together at last. But Anna's practised, involved eye, lingering over the contours of it, detected a new humanity lurking behind the familiar forcefulness. She breathed a tiny sigh of relief. No, she had not misjudged her tactics, nor miscalculated their outcome. Neil's attitude might suggest one thing, but his real message was there in the light from his eyes, the gentler curve of his firm mouth, and she read it as clearly as banner headlines.

This still left her, however, with an unknown quantity. Did he consider this an end, or more like a beginning? After the intensity of these last weeks, did he intend to follow up their embryonic relationship, or had it become too complex and clinical? Did he feel, as she did, the stirrings of something real and deep; or had he simply been using mutual sexual attraction as a lever through the rigours of the case?

All at once Anna was in the grip of an obscure terror, rigid with tension. The worst of it was a total inability to understand herself. Which did she dread most: the thought of seeing him again away from the security of this environment, or the prospect of never seeing him again at all, now she'd served her official purpose?

She took refuge from this sudden flood of bewilderment by turning her back on him to rummage among the papers on her desk for the relevant form. 'I'm glad you came in, Neil.' She kept her voice steady and dispassionate. 'We've got one or two logistical points to . . .'

He was across the room in three strides to stand behind her, hands descending to lie heavy on her shoulders, breath much too close to her ear and stirring in her glossy dark hair, so that she froze in midsentence, clutching the forms against her chest, paralysed at this unexpected onslaught on her senses.

'Anna!' His voice was very low, so near it seemed almost to be coming from her own body. 'Damn logistics! I've kept my hands hands off you for nine weeks, God knows how. I've been a model of virtue and patience; if you knew me better, you'd know just how much patience it's needed to keep up such a level of virtue.' The sardonic mutter was all but lost against the back of her neck. 'But I'm flesh and blood, and I refuse to say or sign another thing until I've reminded myself—reminded us both,' he amended huskily, 'what we've been sacrificing in such a good cause.'

Then he was swivelling her slowly, deliberately, round in his grasp until she faced him, still speechless, still clutching her papers. Gently he removed them from her inert fingers and laid them on the desk behind her, before they became crumpled out of recognition. Gently he cupped her chin in one hand, lifting her hypnotised face up to his. Gently his lips discovered the softness of her mouth, tentatively at first, then with increasing pressure as her instincts rose to meet the demands of his.

Those long weeks had been a dream, a suspension of one reality while she had spent all her energies on another. Now this reality crashed back into focus, an avalanche tearing through her mind and emotions, as Neil gathered the power effortlessly into his own strong hands again. Anna made no complaint, put up no struggle, because at that moment she was nothing but a mass of pure feminine acceptance, matching his strident need with an equal one of her own. She wound her arms about his neck and clenched her fingers in his hair, cleaving to him, pulling him closer. Yet again, here in the unlikely and unsuitable atmosphere of her consulting room, she was letting this man take her over; and not just suffering him to, but urging him to, imploring him to, and exulting in every joyful second of his dominance.

At last, abruptly and yet reluctantly, he released her and stepped back, catching hold of both her hands as his eyes searched her dazed features: the parted lips, the tousled hair, the shining eyes and flushed cheeks. Everything she felt, everything he had awakened within her, glowed now in her face; and Neil smiled as he saw it. Anna had never seen a smile like it, redolent of fierce satisfaction, a possessive, primeval potency. Unconsciously she shivered, and Neil caught her into his arms and held her close against his warm hard body for a full minute, silent but rich in communication.

If she had just been lit up by the sensual touch of him, she was even more deeply ensnared now. This was closeness of another kind: profound, subtle, flowing between the two of them, unhurried and timeless. This was a new warmth that welled up from a new level, a bond that went beyond the simply sexual. In a flash of realisation Anna understood something she had hitherto known only in her head: you could become hooked on a person physically, but it would never last; accompanied by this extraordinary feeling it became a tangible emotion and that person became as indispensable to you as part of your own body.

The understanding filled her with a rush of alarm,

and she stiffened in his arms and pushed him away, moving out of reach of his magnetic force. When she felt safer, she confronted him gravely, ran a steadying but ineffectual hand through her untidy hair and picked up the forms from the desk.

'About these,' she began, feeling slightly foolish but clearing the croak out of her voice, determined to regain her equilibrium, 'we really have got to get them out of the way, and I—we mustn't keep Chris waiting too long . . .' she pointed out, rather desperately.

Neil made no attempt to follow her to her haven behind the desk, but stood watching her laconically as she bustled and blustered. Then his intense features broke into a grin, and irony crept into his tone again. 'Don't panic, flower. I'm not about to attack you again. Not yet, anyway. Just—what shall we say?—staking my claim? Establishing my territory? I apologise if the moment was inconvenient, Anna.' The flippant note hardened, revealing serious depth beneath. 'It's been a long time. I didn't see why I should wait another minute.'

'Not exactly inconvenient,' she muttered, avoiding his gaze as she reached for a pen. 'Just unexpected.'

Neil moved over to the desk, and they faced each other across its surface yet again. His gaze seemed fixed now, intent on her mouth, which trembled in recognition and recollection, setting off chain reactions through the rest of her body. 'Surely not exactly unexpected?' he murmured. 'Not really, Anna? You knew as well as I did that all of it was still there underneath, biding its time, waiting for its chance?'

Anna stared blankly at him, feeling foolish and immature. Had she known, really? She couldn't say, and that was the truth. She was such an expert in subduing and sublimating that side of her nature, concentrating everything into her busy mind, she simply could not be sure whether she had known or not.

She shook her head vigorously as if to clear away confusing dust, and sat down, thrusting the form across

the desk towards him. 'If you could just sign here,
please, Neil,' she ordered briskly. 'And there are one or
two things I'm supposed to say to you before we can
close this file once and for all.' Refusing to look him in
the eye, she stacked some documents together, opened a
drawer and shut it again.

He surveyed her for a few seconds, quizzical; then he
sat down, leaned over to sign the form with a flourish,
and folded his hands in his lap, satirically obedient. 'I'm
all ears,' he announced meekly.

Anna braced herself, linked her fingers together on the
desk top and finally met his gaze directly. Her prepared
speech consisted basically of a succinct summing-up of
the official report she was putting in about Christopher,
and her formal opinion of his situation as it now stood
in relation to the authorities. Neil listened intently,
punctuating his thoughtful silence with an occasional
intelligent nod or grunt of comprehension.

When he knew she had finished he leaned back, still
perusing her but permitting a glint of humour to return
to his eyes. 'This is all admirably clear and concise,
thank you, Dr Coleman. I can find no fault with it, no
quibbles about your perceptive account of Chris's case;
not even my small part in it.' He leaned forward, one
elbow on the desk. 'And now it only remains for me to
offer my official thanks for your skilful ministrations on
our behalf. Christopher and I wish to place our eternal
gratitude on record.' He paused, and she stared at him
dubiously. Was he entirely serious, or was he mocking
her? Even now, even with all her experience of human
nature, he had the ability to keep her guessing as no one
else ever had.

Entirely aware of her uncertainty, he smiled and
allowed himself to end it. 'I mean every word of it,
Anna,' he assured her emphatically. 'Chris and I both
think you're wonderful. What's more, we've got every
intention of keeping up the good work you've started.
Go on,' he added, as she looked away, reddening under
his close scrutiny and his sincere praise, 'write that
down, too. Make a note of it.'

His smile had the impact, at that moment, of a physical gesture, releasing Anna's tension and sparking off her own smile in return. 'I've enjoyed helping Chris,' she heard herself telling Neil truthfully, 'and you've been wonderful, too. None of it would have worked out without you. You know that.' A new confidence permeated her tone as she climbed on to safer, more familiar ground.

'Right. Enough of this mutual admiration society.' Deliberately lightening the atmosphere, Neil glanced at his heavy wristwatch and got to his feet. 'I'd better get out of your way; time to pick up Chris and go.'

Anna stood up too, her heart sinking, shocked at his sudden withdrawal. 'Yes, it's time you did.' What next? What would he say next? Would he just leave things hanging there, or . . .?

'Aren't you forgetting something?' Neil accused sharply, but amusement was twitching a corner of his mouth.

'Forgetting?' Anna frowned, puzzled, taken aback.

'Your side of our bargain?'

'Bargain?' She felt distinctly stupid, echoing his words like this, but he had caught her on the hop.

'My proposed work of art? My television documentary? The one you're thinking about helping me with—the one you've been considering all these weeks, ready to leap into frenzied action the moment our case was completed? Your little bribe?'

'Ah!' Anna bit her lip, recalling it only too well. '*That* bargain!'

'That's the one!' Neil whistled through his teeth, ostentatiously awaiting her reply. When none came, he pressed on. 'My forbearance has even extended to not bringing the subject up the whole time we were reporting for duty here. Or perhaps,' he suggested sarcastically, 'you hadn't noticed?'

'Of course I noticed!' Her hot denial was only partly true, in fact: while it lasted, Anna's commitment to any case was always total. But somewhere underneath she had remembered, and she had noticed. 'Now that the case is over I've got to consult my senior colleague. I'm pretty sure it'll be okay, Neil,' she said carefully, 'but I can't say now.'

'I see.' His expression had hardened, and she could hardly blame him. After everything he had given during these demanding weeks, the least he deserved was a positive response. But there was more to it than that: whether or not she would risk further regular contact with him, for a start. She had to think it through a bit longer. 'Well, let me know when you come up with a definite answer, Anna, so that I can look elsewhere if necessary.' *You've had long enough*, his tone implied; but he, too, had learned a lot in their sessions, and he kept his criticism unspoken. 'I'm much too interested in the subject to let it escape the Tyrell treatment.'

This new quality in him of calm acceptance reached out to Anna, loosening some deeper inhibitions. On an impulse she came round the desk to lay an expressive hand on his arm. 'Of course I'll let you know, very soon. I'd like to do it, Neil. I've just got to sort out a few problems first.'

He stared down into her face, his own features softening. As if realising with a high-voltage shock where it was, her hand tingled against the bare brown skin of his muscular forearm in its rolled-up shirtsleeve. She snatched it away and tucked it under her other arm, and Neil smiled broadly as he registered the action. 'I'll look forward to hearing from you then, Anna—when you're ready for me.' The phrase carried a double edge: he was making his point, leaving the initiative to her in more ways than one, and she knew it. 'You know where to find me, if you want me.'

'Yes, Neil.' Anna walked to the door, opened it, and stood aside to let him through. 'I know where you are, and I'll be in touch when I've decided.'

'Don't 'phone us, eh?' He paused in the open doorway, still smiling faintly down at her, one fair brow arched. Then he was striding past her, brushing very lightly against her as he went, flinging a final 'Thanks again!' over his shoulder before disappearing along the corridor to his waiting brother.

The very next day, Anna presented herself in Daniel's consulting room before they both went home. It was one of those glorious high summer afternoons, not far from the longest day, which promise to last forever. Sun streamed in through all the windows of the clinic, highlighting dusty air, threadbare floors, fading colours; causing staff and clients alike to wonder what they were doing in there at all rather than outside enjoying this rare golden British weather.

Daniel's bushy grey head was bent over his chaotic desk, but he looked up to grin as Anna came in and sat down, patiently waiting while he finished writing some notes.

'Bloody paper-pushing,' he grumbled. 'All I ever seem to do in this place.' It was far from true, as they both knew perfectly well, but Anna merely smiled. To her own surprise, she was quite content to stare out at the incredible dense blue of the sky. She wished it would stop reminding her of the colour of Neil's eyes, but then life in general seemed to be conspiring to keep her thoughts running on the man to an extent that was little short of clinically obsessive . . .

'Now then, Anna.' She jumped as Daniel, who had put down his pen some while ago, drew her wandering attention for the second time. 'What can I do for you today?'

She dragged herself back to earth. 'It's about the Tyrell case.'

'Ah yes; from what I've gathered you've got that one tidily wrapped up. Social welfare reports are glowing, and the file reads like a study in how to run successful Family Therapy. How did you manage it, Anna?' He beetled at her under his thick brows. 'Looked like a tough one, that older brother, but you obviously brought him to heel.'

Which of them had brought which to heel was a matter for debate, but Anna wasn't pursuing that line of thought. 'It wasn't difficult at all, once we'd established common ground.' She found she was fighting to suppress a blush which threatened to creep up from her neck as she groped for words which did not carry a potential double meaning. 'He was very highly motivated and determined, once I'd convinced him of the necessity for his total involvement.'

'Good, good!' Beneath his cheery bluster, Daniel was observing her shrewdly as usual, picking up every nuance of tone and expression. 'Knew you could do it! So, what's your problem now, if it's all tied up?'

'Not exactly a problem,' she explained. 'Not about the case, as such. But I need to ask your advice. You see, the only way I managed to persuade him to come back, when he looked like deserting the case, was by striking a sort of bargain with him. Neil, that is,' she added, in case that wasn't abundantly clear.

'Bargain?' The shaggy brows lifted. This sounded more interesting than ever: Daniel had suspected hidden ramifications in this stormy confrontation between his young colleague and her most difficult client—or rather, client's relative—but there appeared to be even more to it than met the eye. Even Daniel's eye. 'What do you mean, bargain?'

So Anna told him all about Neil's job, and his proposed television programme; about his request that she help him piece it together, provide professional advice and support, compile suitable material for real and simulated example cases ... and as she told him, her eyes lit up and her voice took on a vibrant warmth. For the first time, she realised just how much she did want to do it—how excited the prospect made her feel—and the realisation both upset and astonished her.

Daniel listened intently, broad palms pressed flat together as if he was praying, a gesture he made when concentrating hard. When she came to an end, he looked her straight in the eye to demand, 'And do you want to do it, Anna?'

'Yes,' she admitted, 'I think I do.'

'So why didn't you just say you would?' he persisted bluntly.

'Because I was involved in the case, of course,' she retorted instantly. 'How could I when we were meeting here twice a week to counsel his brother? And then, when the case was closed and he asked me again, I said I must consult you first, in case it wasn't professionally . . .'

'Ethical?' Daniel waved a dismissive hand. 'We've been through all this already, Anna. Going to lunch with the man wasn't going to be ethical either, remember?' She remembered only too well; and little did Daniel know just how unethical that occasion had turned out to be! 'Now,' he leaned forward, earnest and emphatic, 'the file's closed, you're keen to do it and I must say I think it sounds fascinating. What's more, it's an excellent chance to publicise some of our methods and practices to the viewing multitudes; and if we're being given our say by an intelligent director, the results might even be accurate and comprehensive for a change.'

'I'm only telling you what I've heard about Neil,' Anna reminded him defensively. 'I don't watch much TV myself.'

Daniel frowned behind his heavy spectacles. 'Come to think of it, I'm pretty sure I've come across his work. I think he did a thing, some years ago, about dreams, covering research into REM sleep—solid, perceptive stuff.' He nodded vehemently. 'Yes, you should do it, Anna, and I'll muscle in on it, too—the psychiatric angle—try keeping me out!' he announced defiantly.

'I told him you'd want to be in on it, and he said the more the merrier,' Anna recalled, with a slight smile which did not escape Daniel's notice.

'Right; well, you just get back to this Tyrell and tell him he has a free hand and our co-operation,' Daniel instructed her sternly. 'We owe it to our trade to grab all the sympathetic and authentic media treatment we can find, eh? God knows, we need it. Get all the gen from him, Anna: how he wants to go about it, what facilities he needs, how much time, all that sort of thing.

Then we can all get together and discuss it, and I can bring in some of our other more illustrious cronies as advisers and frontmen. Front*persons*,' he corrected with a chuckle. Daniel was like a creative, energetic steamroller: once his imagination was captured there was no stopping him. His enthusiasm was infectious, but Anna reserved some caution.

'So, you want me to talk to him first, prepare the ground?'

'Who else? You're the one who knows him,' Daniel pointed out blandedly. 'No use skirting it, Anna, you've got to get together. Don't worry, it's quite safe,' he teased, 'you no longer have a professional relationship. Go out to dinner,' he ordered airily, 'ask him over; do what you like, but do it. Have a good long talk about his ideas. I shall expect you to come back to me well-briefed,' he warned. 'I'm far too busy to lay the groundwork myself.'

She stared at him, trying to read his expression. Was that a gleam in his eyes or simply the sunlight glinting off his lenses? She was supposed to be the pschologist, but Daniel could be inscrutable when he chose. Was he really pushing her, cleverly encouraging her into Neil's dangerous orbit, for reasons of his own—or was that just a paranoid suspicion on her part?

She shrugged, grinned and gave it up as a bad job. Whatever the outcome, she could take care of herself: she was a mature woman, made her own choices. Daniel was right to demand that she open herself to a few risks on behalf of their professions. It might even turn out to be a rewarding experience.

'All right, Daniel,' she said firmly. 'I'll do it. Leave it with me.'

He returned her grin. 'Well done, Anna. Let me know what we do next.' He stretched his sturdy frame and yawned luxuriously. 'And now it's high time we got out of this stuffy place and into what's left of that sunshine. I've had more than enough for one week, and I'm damn sure you have, too.'

*   *   *

That evening, spurred into an unaccustomed boldness by Daniel's subtle challenge, Anna telephoned Neil from home to tell him she was agreeing to his request, and furthermore that her senior colleague was not only willing but eager to involve himself and his considerable skill and knowledge in the project. She kept her tone cool and businesslike, but it was almost impossible not to echo the clear delight that rang in Neil's immediate response to the news.

'That's great, Anna! I can't wait to tell you my plans. I've got a list of ideas as long as both your arms. When can we meet? And where?'

He sounded pleased, though not exactly surprised. Obviously, Anna's mind reflected drily, he must have been fairly sure of her eventual affirmative decision. Before she lost the impetus which had induced her to dial his number in the first place, she found herself inviting coolly, 'Why don't you come over to supper with me here, and we can talk about it?'

This time, when Neil's voice came back to her, surprise rendered it deeper and more resonant, almost cutting through her armour of efficiency. 'Supper with you, at your flat? Are you sure?'

'Why not?' she countered breezily. 'It would appear to be my turn to feed you.'

'I wasn't aware we were taking turns,' he remarked. 'But I'm not complaining. Just tell me the time and place and I'll report for duty.'

'Duty?' Safe at the end of a few miles of telephone line, Anna risked a slightly daring dig. 'Is that what it is?'

'Okay then.' There was a smile in his voice. 'Business. And any business conducted with you, Dr Coleman,' he asserted, 'will be a pleasure.'

Briskly she gave him her address. 'Shall we say next Saturday, at eight?'

'Next Saturday it is. Shall I bring any contributions?'

'Certainly not.' She affected outrage at the suggestion. 'Just yourself. And your list of ideas, of course; wouldn't be much point in coming without that.'

'Oh, I don't know.' The cryptic observation seemed fraught with implications.

Anna decided it was time she dragged the conversation on to neutral ground. 'How's Chris today?'

'Absolutely fine. He gets better every day. Mrs R thinks you should be deified, or at the very least beatified. The name of Anna Coleman is revered in this house,' Neil informed her in hushed tones.

Anna giggled, but she was beginning to feel slightly unnerved by what she had just done: inviting Neil Tyrell over to her home for an evening, indeed! Daniel must have goaded her into even more of an ebullient mood than she had realised; wretched man, with his mind-bending tricks, even if it was with good reason . . .

But it was too late to backtrack now, and suddenly she was exhausted, longing only for a peaceful weekend and lots of lovely cooking. She brought their exchange to an abrupt end with a convenient—and probably transparent—lie. 'Must go now, Neil, someone at the door. See you next weekend.'

'A week tomorrow,' he confirmed. 'See you then, Anna.'

'Goodbye, Neil.' She replaced the receiver slowly in its cradle and then sat for a long time, staring blankly at it.

Inside her the battle raged, bewildering surges of elation and dread, hope and fear. Would they ever settle down and leave her in tranquillity again?

CHAPTER NINE

THE following week wore inexorably on. Anna found it ridiculously difficult to keep her mind on the demanding routines of daily life, or on anything other than the rapidly approaching weekend. She seemed to have become a stranger to herself. How could she come to terms with this impulsive, even brazen, young woman who had spontaneously agreed to involve herself in Neil's scheme—and therefore, by implication, with the man himself? Who had quite gratuitously invited him to her flat for an evening? True, a less-than-subtle prod from Daniel had eased her in that direction, damn him; but it was hardly fair to blame her colleague. If she was honest with herself, every instinct had led her the same way.

By midweek she was in a confused lather, wrenched virtually in half by the twin forces of anticipation and apprehension. In three days' time Neil was going to present himself on her doorstep, expecting an intimate evening *à deux*, some productive conversation, a meal, and who knew what more personal levels of communication? Her insides churned every time she contemplated it, which was frequently; but when she analysed her feelings, the churnings felt more like excitement than anxiety.

What should she do? Cancel it, or see it through? Oh, she wanted to see it through, very much indeed. Her real self knew that what she wanted more than anything else in the world was to spend some hours alone, uninterrupted and on a strictly unprofessional basis with Neil Tyrell. There was no way she could get round that stark fact. It was bald, undeniable. Try as she might to evade it, in the dark sleepless night hours, it crept back through all her elaborate barriers as easily as sunshine through iron railings, rendering them so futile as to be positively laughable.

Keeping her wits about her as far as possible, she tried to counsel herself, to search deep inside herself as if she was one of her own clients. It proved painful and difficult, but she pushed herself to do it, and she succeeded. She was so used to dividing her active mind off from her emotions that the merging together of the two creaked and jarred like an old machine grinding into rusty action. But Anna was too intelligent and self-aware to turn back once she had started. Ruthless with herself, just as she was with clients, she laid bare the areas which had been so carefully covered for so long.

It was quite simple really, once she got down to it. Paper qualifications in psychology were hardly necessary in order to perceive her inner shape and how it had got that way. She felt foolish, schizoid, realising just how far she had been kidding herself, and for how long. But underneath the negative feelings were new positive ones, the stirring of a fresh freedom ahead— still vague, but elating.

Through those long nights, Anna forced herself to recall her lonely childhood with its atmosphere so strongly steeped in intellectual prowess that no other level of achievement was possible. The only real response she had ever earned from her cool, cerebral parents was as a result of academic distinction. Inevitably, she had grown up incapable of risking warm physical relationships in case she was rejected; in case she failed to come up to scratch mentally and failed the test as a valid, lovable person in her own right. All her adult life she had worked and worked at winning the approval of the adult world, even once she was clearly part of it, in the subconscious hope of indirectly winning her own parents' approval at last. Since human closeness was out of the question until she had succeeded, the only way was by furthering her career. If she became a brilliant success in that context, surely nothing else could matter? In the process she had become used to spurning every tentative suggestion of true emotional commitment. She had closed herself off from the most important area of human activity. The irony of it was, she was always lecturing her own clients about not doing just that; but she had managed to practise the opposite of what she preached, and it had torn her apart until she operated on two distinct levels, running in parallel lines which never met.

Until now. Neil Tyrell, with his own strength of will and honest self-discovery, had opened up some pathway into her, forced those parallel lines to bend until they met and created a turmoil within her so that order became chaos, and then a new order formed out of the chaos: a vibrant blend of rationality, feelings and sensuality. Whether he himself followed it up or not, there was no point in fighting it: she knew that. Anna had became a hibernating animal, suddenly awake. She had to pay heed to her natural rhythms and urges as sure as a tree has to put on its new leaves.

Anna was a decisive person. Once she had reached this understanding she knew her life could never return to its old blinkered patterns. She had been on the right track, chasing a good instinct, in asking Neil to her flat. Daniel knew it, too. For years Daniel had been trying to tell her how barren her personal life was, and how badly it affected her professional life. She had chosen to disregard his hints, on the grounds that the subject was none of his business; now she recognised them as affectionately and accurately offered.

The way was clear ahead of her. She had a lot to learn, to catch up on, and she was consumed with a fervent mixture of joy and fear at the prospect of learning it at the hands of Neil Tyrell. They were experienced hands, he had said so himself. And she was nervous and uncertain, a novice: what if those hands let her down, and she got badly hurt? Why should he want to be the one to teach her? Perhaps his own interest in her was less personal and more practical than he had led her to think? Perhaps, she tortured herself, he only wanted what he could get out of her, never intended her to be any more than those other women he had allowed into the edges of his life ... milking her for what she

was worth professionally, and now (she winced)
sexually? How could she find out, if not the hard way?

There was no other way, she decided boldly. It was a
risk she had to run, if she was to carry through her new
acceptance of reality, vulnerability. She would have to
cope somehow. She was (why not put an honest label
on it?) in love with the man. Her own feelings left her
no choice but to follow where they led her.

On the strength of this determination, she spent much
of Saturday in an orgy of happy creativity in her
kitchen, leaving only forty minutes in which to bath and
change. At exactly two minutes past eight she opened
the door to Neil, still pink and tingling from the scented
water, her dark hair damply curling, her skin glowing.
It was a balmy evening and she had worn a cool outfit:
a filmy harem suit in shades of rich, deep red, threaded
with gold strands, gathered at wrists and ankles, softly
flowing to disguise and yet reveal her rounded form; her
feet in simple leather thongs.

Neil, in lean navy cords and jacket, grey-blue shirt
open at the neck, thick blond mane slightly neater than
usual, flourished a tissue-wrapped bottle in one hand
and a small potted plant in the other.

'Didn't see you as a cut-flower person,' he announced
without preamble, the moment she stood before him,
'but I thought you might be a begonia person?'

Swallowing a sudden constriction in her throat, Anna
took the plant and lifted it up to have a good look. 'It's
beautiful, Neil; thank you. You're quite right, I am a
begonia person. Come in and see for yourself.'

She led him through the tiny hall into the simply
furnished, airy main room, sash windows open at the
top tonight to catch the slight breeze. As if to illustrate
her point, each shelf and occasional table sported its
healthy collection of potted plants jostling for position.
She set the begonia down next to a thriving scented
geranium, heady on the evening air, then took him into
the kitchen where she waved a hand at the window
ledge crowded with cacti and succulents of all shapes,
sizes and degrees of prickliness.

'You see?' She turned to face him. 'I'm a plant person.'

He studied her gravely, deep blue gaze travelling slowly, pleasurably, from her face to her feet and then back again. Then he smiled, and it was like a physical contact. 'Of course you are; you had to be.' He handed her the bottle. 'I hope you're a Liebfraumilch person as well?'

'Love it; thanks, Neil.' Her fingers trembled a little as she tore off the tissue paper and put the bottle in her small fridge. 'This'll go perfectly with the Tandoori Chicken. I'd got some beer in, but this is much nicer. But first,' she turned away from those intense eyes, 'come and have a drink. It won't be long.'

But there was no evading the eyes: they drilled into the back of her as she led the way to the sitting-room, just as they had registered the front, missing nothing. And for the first time in her life Anna did not cringe at such direct scrutiny, but held her head high and walked with her natural jaunty gait, challenging Neil to think what he would, showing that she was conscious of his appreciation.

She poured him a cold beer and herself an iced orange juice, and took them over to where he stood staring out at the beginnings of a summer dusk. 'It may be grotty round here,' he remarked, without looking round, 'but this is a nice flat, and you've got yourself a great little view.'

'That's why I chose the flat, among other things.' She set the drinks down on a small table and joined him at the window. 'At least it gives me a sense of space.' She pointed out to one side. 'You can see Hampstead Heath—see—that's Parliament Hill. And the other way you can just make out the dome of St Paul's among all those skyscrapers.'

They surveyed it together for a minute or so, without speaking. 'London,' Neil mused. Then he swung round to face her, brows interrogatively arched. 'Do you like living in London, Anna?'

'Most of the time. It would be lovely to get out more often,' she admitted.

'I've been thinking of buying a place in the country.' It was almost as if he was talking to himself, working it out.

'What, moving away?' Anna hoped she didn't sound as disturbed as she felt at the prospect.

'Couldn't do that, no, not permanently. I must have a home base here. No, I thought just a cottage, somewhere remote to disappear to between times, you know . . . roses round the door, a vista of fields, all that stuff. Perhaps,' he added, fixing her with his eyes, 'near the sea.'

'Isle of Wight?' Anna ventured, taking an instant calculated risk.

For a moment he hesitated, and she read the pain that flitted across his expressive features. Then he grinned, and she breathed a sigh of relief. 'I think not, Anna. Perhaps Dorset, or Devon; I love the West Country. What do you think?'

She took a step away, reaching for her drink. 'Does it make any difference what I think? Either of those places would be wonderful, and I'm sure Chris . . .'

He grabbed her arm before she could pick up her glass, twisting her round and pulling her back to his side. 'It might make a difference. You might get invited to my rural retreat for weekends or holidays. Wouldn't you like that, Anna?'

A harsh quality had permeated his tone, and his fingers bit into the tender flesh of her upper arm, but she faced up to him squarely. 'I'd like that, of course, Neil. It's a very tempting thought, especially in this sort of weather. It's been so warm recently . . .'

'Come on now, flower,' he almost sneered, as his left hand came up to catch hold of her other arm, effectively pinioning her. 'I'm not here to talk about the weather, great British institution though it may be. You and I have got better fish to fry.'

'Chicken, actually.' Hazel eyes steady on his face, Anna made a stab at a corny joke to defuse a situation which was already becoming super-charged, danger-ously early. For all her resolutions, Anna almost gave way to a wave of sheer, sick panic.

'Funny lady.' But Neil was not laughing: he was drawing her towards him, releasing her arms and gathering her tightly against him, letting his hands range freely up and down her back and around her hips, running sensitive fingers the length of her spine, arousing shivers and tremors all the way through her frame.

'Neil . . .' At first she stood rigid, resentful; but gradually the warmth of his power flowed into her, and she melted against him and was lost. Her own hands crept round his broad back; she revelled once again in this merging, this fusing, this heat which the two of them seemed to generate so magically.

He broke away just far enough to bring his lips down to hers. The kiss they shared was a light tasting, a tantalising: a hint and a promise. Then Anna drew her mouth away, lifted her right hand and laid the fingers on his lips. 'Neil,' she murmured, as he caught one of her fingertips and nibbled it between his teeth, 'we've got things to talk about, remember? And don't you want any supper?'

He chuckled. 'Not Hard-hearted Hannah, but Hard-headed Anna. Okay.' Letting her go, he stepped back to the window, his eyes and mouth softened, almost dreamy as he resumed his gaze over the rooftops. 'You bring on the food and I'll make with the business conference. Feed the body, exercise the brain.' He picked up his tankard and took a long swig of beer, as if to steady himself.

Anna carried her orange juice into the kitchen, where she mixed the salad and took the sizzling chicken and the fresh *nan*—puffy ovals of hot Indian bread—out of the oven. Then she arranged it all on platters and took it through to the small dining table, ready laid at one corner of the main room. Disappearing back to the kitchen, she returned with the Liebfraumilch and a corkscrew, both of which she presented ceremoniously to Neil as he came over to join her.

'Do something intelligent with these,' she instructed, 'and then we can eat.'

His expression became sardonic. 'So, it's the heavy work, the real brute force job?' He smiled, pushing back the lock of fair hair that fell over his high forehead, reminding Anna all at once of Christopher. 'Before I engage myself in such manly pursuits,' he entreated, 'may I have your permission to remove my jacket?'

'You have my permission.' Anna returned the smile. 'In fact I wish you would. It makes me feel hot just looking at it.'

Neil hung the cord jacket over his chair, rolled up his shirtsleeves, flexed his muscles like a strongman at a sideshow, smoothly uncorked the bottle and poured two glassfuls with panache. Then he sat watching Anna as she dished the red-gold pieces of chicken on to plates. 'That looks fantastic.' He sniffed appreciatively. 'It's one of my favourites, but I've never had it outside an Indian restaurant.' He shot her a sly glance. 'Obviously, Dr Coleman, you're a lady of many skilful parts.'

'I like to think so,' Anna assured him breezily as she handed the salad and bread.

'I never doubted it. And I have every intention of learning more about all of them.' He raised his glass. 'To our mutual projects, Anna. May they prosper!'

'May they prosper,' she repeated, something in her body responding to the cryptic toast: the tone in which it had been spoken, rather than the words themselves. A little feverishly, she sipped the refreshingly chilled white wine.

While they ate, Neil outlined his thoughts and plans about the proposed documentary, and Anna became more and more fascinated. There was no doubt that she and Daniel, with carefully selected colleagues, would be able to supply enough suitable material for Neil to work into stunning viewing with a clear, concise theme. This, he took pains to explain, was what he wanted: a combination of factual accuracy with instant emotional effect. It was no good working in a visual medium if you sacrificed one of those to the other. Both were vital if you were to create good television.

Anna listened, absorbed, occasionally throwing a suggestion or reaction of her own into the ring, and Neil treated each one seriously, obviously delighted that she understood exactly what he was aiming at. They completed their meal with one of Anna's home-made raspberry sorbets; then Neil produced a notebook and pen from his jacket pocket and sat down on the sofa with them, while Anna went into the kitchen to brew strong coffee. He was scribbling furiously when she came back, so she kept quiet, putting the tray down on the low table and shutting the windows against the cooling, darkening air. Then she came back to sit in the armchair opposite him, mesmerised by the fluency of bold black strokes on white paper.

Without pausing or raising his head, he addressed her. 'What's the matter? Gone off me?' He patted the sofa cushions next to him with his free hand. 'Come and sit here.' It was more of an order than an invitation, but Anna found herself complying meekly. At once his arm was around her, her head resting on his shoulder. It felt so easy, so normal, she wondered what on earth she'd been afraid of.

Neil continued writing for another minute, then put the notebook and pen on the table and nuzzled his cheek against the top of her hair. It seemed to Anna that time froze while they sat together, a tableau of peace and empathy, needing no words. How good it would have been just to sit there like that for ever! To push all those thoughts, those cluttering considerations of everyday life, out of the way, just concentrating on the cocoon that was this moment!

'How about this coffee, then?' Neil stretched both legs out in front of him and both arms along the back of the sofa, smiling down at her.

'Oh yes, sorry,' she mumbled, jerked back to reality, feeling suddenly foolish. She leaned over to pour it out and hand him a cup. He took it, and she moved away so that she could pour and sip hers. All at once brittle and embarrassed, she avoided his eye as he studied her over the rim.

'Tell me about yourself, Anna,' he demanded brusquely into the dense silence, making her jump so that she almost spilled the remains of her coffee into the saucer.

'What about myself?' She was defensive now, anxious. 'You know most of it.'

'On the contrary, I don't know a thing, except what I can see for myself, and I'd like to know a whole lot more. Family, for instance. Parents, sisters, brothers? After all,' he paused reflectively, 'you know everything there is to know about mine. It seems only fair, if we're to conduct our future relationship on equal terms.'

She glanced suspiciously up at him, but he seemed perfectly serious. His own armour, that daunting streak of irony, had apparently been laid aside for once. So she told him, rather reluctantly, about her parents and her solitary childhood, as succinctly as possible. It all sounded cold and stark compared to the emotional richness of Neil's early life, despite the tough years at boarding school.

Neil was evidently engrossed. 'So you hardly ever see them now?' She shook her head. 'That seems sad, Anna.' He was oddly vehement. 'If you're lucky enough to still have parents, you should make the most of it.'

She stared at him. 'I've never thought of it like that before. I told you, they aren't exactly warm and supportive. We've got so little in common. They don't seem very keen to see me, either. They've always been more interested,' she observed bitterly, 'in what I *do* than what I *am*.'

'You can't tell, if you don't try.' He shrugged, then smiled again. 'Go on, tell me it's none of my bloody business how you conduct your life.' Anna had been going to say no such thing. In fact he had made her think quite hard. There was no point in resenting them for the people they had been when she was a child; perhaps he was right, and she should make the effort to get to know them all over again, as free and equal adults . . . especially now that she was breaking out of the cage they had helped to put her in . . . 'What about other commitments?' Neil was saying, his expression changing to teasing curiosity. 'I can see you live alone at the moment, but I can't believe you don't have—liaisons?'

Anna stared straight ahead, her colour rising. 'I haven't had much time for "liaisons" outside work,' she commented stiffly.

'Pull the other one!' His eyes widened as he affected disbelief. 'A lovely woman like you without admirers! All that passion . . .' his voice dropped as he slid closer, allowing his arm to rest behind her shoulders again, 'and nowhere to aim it?'

'I like to keep to myself,' she declared candidly, wishing it sounded less empty. 'And I've never needed . . . never wanted it any different . . .' She stared down into her lap, the words trailing into a husky whisper, unable to explain fully just then.

'I somehow can't believe,' he murmured, very close, his hold tightening, 'that I'm about to wade in and change the chaste habits of a lifetime.'

Anna opened her mouth, but no sound emerged. Here they were, the two of them, in a situation which could only be described as compromising and which she had been at least equally responsible for creating; his body transmitting messages which were surely as old as the human race itself, and yet which carried an urgency that only this moment could answer . . . her body responding in every fibre of it . . . so how could she refute his claim? It must look unlikely, even impossible, that a mature woman so obviously equipped with all the correct instincts could be so utterly inexperienced.

She turned towards him so that she could meet his eye and deny his challenge outright; but the instant she did so, she knew it was pointless. In that second she gave up all pretence at control or deception, surrendering the power to him with an audible sigh of release. And then she was lying back, and Neil was supporting his body on one elbow, the full firm length of it pressed close to hers, but keeping his head raised so that he could stare down into her face and drink in her volatile expressions: dazed uncertainty, dawning wonder, heedless desire.

After that she knew nothing except the sweetness of what he did to her, each new sensation he taught her, all the surging emotions he tapped in her at the simple touch of fingers, lips, tongue. Her mind blanked out at last to a wordless streak of red as he sought her out, first through the soft layer of cotton, then burrowing beneath it, pushing aside obstacles with a gentle determination which expected no protest and found none. In fact she willed him on, conducting her own pleasurable explorations of his lines and sinews, delighting in the silky sensuality of her hands on his taut, hot skin.

He had uncovered and discovered the pale smooth roundness of her breasts, and was relishing them, teasing them until she gasped aloud and clasped him to her in a rising frenzy. Even her wildest, most illicit dreams had never imagined this delicious agony, this craving which could only be satisfied by more and yet more of the same. This longing, born of him and which only he had the power to fulfil. And now his mouth was taking over as his hands pushed the zip of her harem suit down, farther down, finding their way into it and round the softness, the curves of her stomach, hips and thighs . . .

For an instant, no more than a split second, Anna stiffened and drew away, her moan of ecstasy laced with alarm, her passionate movements edged with a brief panic. She sensed a watershed, a point of no return, and she reacted beyond thought, impulsively, as anyone would who was about to make a leap into the unknown. Even as she paused, there was no doubt about her decision: to go on, to follow her instinct, not to stop there. But it was too late. Neil was not so lost in his own needs and urges that he failed to keep in tune with hers. At once his sensitive antennae were alerted, and he halted, pulled back from her, detached himself both physically and mentally so that he could gaze down into her face.

Flushed, his breathing ragged, his body clearly crying out for hers, he retained control nonetheless. As soon as he read the fleeting expression in her eyes, his own hardened and he drew even farther away, running an agitated hand through his dishevelled hair to steady himself. 'Anna! What in hell's name . . .?'

Totally disorientated, far too wrapped in emotion and sensation to understand what was going on, Anna could only stare back at him, her hands still reaching out for him, her arms empty, her desire already turning to frustration even as she sensed his withdrawal. 'What's the matter?' she managed to stutter, on a whisper.

Suddenly, unaccountably, he was fierce and hostile. 'I might ask you the same question.' He began to fasten buttons, tucking his shirt into his jeans, his profile harsh in the dim light.

'But I . . . nothing's wrong . . . Neil, I wanted it, too.' She was astonished at her own boldness, but it was no more than the truth and this was no time for coyness. 'Neil!' In a flood of fear, she laid a hand on his arm. 'What did I do wrong?'

He reached over to do up her zip, tenderly, without passion, his anger abating. 'That's just it, Anna—you don't know. You don't know what you were doing, do you?'

She shook her head, lost and bewildered. Surely it had been there, it had been right for them both; surely she hadn't been the only one to feel how perfect it was?

He was even smiling a little now as he recovered his composure. 'You were telling me the truth, weren't you, Anna? Earlier, when you said you'd never had— affairs?' She nodded, unable to deny it but still wondering why it mattered so much. 'I hit the nail on the head, didn't I, when I joked about changing the chaste habits of a lifetime?' he pressed, his voice deep and earnest, his eyes a darkening blue. She nodded again, wordless. 'Well, don't you see what a difference it makes? I can't just—just barge in here and grab what you have to give. I can't . . . I don't . . . I'm not in the habit,' he stated with grim precision, 'of despoiling pristine goods, just for the sake of it. Deflowering innocent virgins,' he emphasised cruelly, in case she had missed the point. 'It might be a game some men play, collecting scalps—for want of a better word,' he added drily, 'but I've never been one of them. If I'm not on an equal basis with a woman, in every respect, I'm not in the business of making use of them.'

'But Neil, I never thought you were!' Anna was out of her depth, only vaguely understanding his agitation. 'If I hadn't wanted it to happen, I wouldn't have . . .'

'No, Anna, I don't suppose you would.' He was calmer now, his gaze searching her face as if he was seeing a new person. 'But—how can I explain it? I'm not ready to take on that responsibility. I didn't come here expecting anything in particular, and I'm glad we had such a successful and useful discussion; but when it comes to this other thing—well, I never realised you were quite so . . .' he chose his words with delicate care, 'untouched. If you can't see that it makes all the difference in the world, I don't know how I can explain it.'

She was beginning to understand his drift, but she could only continue to stare at him like a stupid schoolgirl, a role she had never played in her life before. Neil tried again. 'You're a beautiful woman, Anna, with everything to offer, and whoever has the privilege of being the first to take it from you, to teach you about yourself, will be a lucky man. But I just don't know . . .' he passed a weary hand over his brow, 'whether it should be me. That's all.'

'I see.' Her voice was low, and she looked away, refusing to meet his eye now that she comprehended him. This was a rejection of a quite unexpected kind; of all the outcomes of tonight's situation she had feverishly envisaged, this had never been among them. 'I expect you're right.' Her tone was dull and flat; she sat rigid.

'I'm sorry, Anna.' Leaning towards her, he touched his fingers briefly to her cheek, rekindling embers which still sparked, causing a confusion of fires to rage within her: passion and anger, regret and shame. 'If it's any comfort, this is a first for me, too. It's never happened to me before.'

'No.' It was little comfort, but at least she wasn't just one in a chain.

He rose, walked over to the chair where he had left his jacket and picked it up. Then he walked over to the door, where he turned and looked across at her for a long painful moment. She could feel his eyes upon her, even though she refused to turn and meet them. 'I'll be in touch, Anna. Perhaps now the case is over—once we get to know each other on more neutral ground, or even on my ground . . . well, maybe we can pick up this scene where we left it. Forgive me if I seem ungallant. It was a lovely meal, and . . .' his voice cracked, 'you're a lovely lady. Don't take it personally. Now I'll go, before· I make things any worse.'

Quietly he let himself out. In the resounding silence, Anna heard the front door slam two floors below, and then the Rover's engine purring smoothly away. For a very long time she sat staring into the vacuum he had left behind; an inner space, always filled in the past with meaningless words and concepts and ideologies, but now bereft of the only thing it wanted to be filled with: the mutual flow of feelings.

Really, if she wasn't near to tears she might almost have laughed. Talk about being hoist with her own petard! All these years she had guarded her virtue along with her heart, waiting till the right person came by—if they ever did—to storm both; and now here he was, and she had never been so sure of anything in her life, and he was refusing to accept the responsibility of her offer!

She had thought she knew as much as there was to know about the complexities of the human mind and spirit, but she was only just beginning to learn. It had been a chastening experience, in more ways than one. She was hurt and she was distressed, but she was made of stronger stuff than to give up now. She refused to be daunted, or avoid further contact with Neil, now that her new alive self was out in the open. She would work with him, let him take over the action, become a satellite in his orbit and a spectator in his arena; play it his way, and see where they went from there.

CHAPTER TEN

NEIL'S thoughts had obviously been running along similar lines. The evening may have ended in fiasco, but at least it had been fruitful otherwise. On Monday morning he was on the telephone, briskly detached, confirming the plans they had drawn up and ensuring that Daniel and Anna were all set to go ahead. No hint, either in his tone or his words, suggested anything more personal. Somehow Anna managed to play along and keep her own voice cool and pragmatic. Just once she almost gave way, breaking into a brief pause with a cautious: 'Neil, about Saturday night . . .'

'It was a superb meal.' He cut her off brusquely.

'I only wanted to say I understand what you were . . .'

'I think, Anna,' his voice came back, gentle but firm, 'the less we say, the better. We reached some useful conclusions about my programme, and that's what I want to concentrate on if you don't mind.'

He exuded a note of authority, and Anna, already tired and subdued, acquiesced to it. Perhaps he was right, after all. There was a job to be done, and they would be involved in it together. They had already proved they could work in harness as long as she held the reins. Neil had shown himself mature and sensitive enough to follow where she led, trusting enough to strip off layers of corrosion from himself under her gentle guidance. Their mental rapport was considerable; their physical one (Anna bit her lip painfully as she forced the recollections through) dynamic. It only remained to be seen whether the all-important emotional dimension was truly there, too. For her, she knew it was; she knew it instinctively, in her bones. But Neil had made it clear that for him, things were far from certain at that level, and only time and patience would tell.

Knowing this, Anna slumped into a kind of automatic drive. Everything functioned adequately on a normal daily plane, but underneath she was almost numb. Only at night and when she was alone at home did her inner self spring into action to torment her with burning regrets, doubts and hopes. Her own trained and newly awakened mind understood perfectly well that there were three distinct layers of her: the outer one, as placid and busy as ever; the second one, clothed still in a protective armour; the inner one, seething turmoil of recently discovered desires, shame, frustration, guilt.

On the Sunday, the day after, she had skulked in her flat, stunned, suspended. She saw no one, and the telephone glared at her in mocking silence. By the end of the afternoon she felt desperate for some company, someone undemanding and easy-going who would soothe and cosset her ego, ply her with coffee and compliments, cheer her and encourage her ... someone right on her doorstep, always there and reliable ...

Who else was she thinking of but Jonathan? Without stopping to change her mind she grabbed her key and her jacket, slammed her door and was downstairs and outside his in half a minute. As usual, the strains of his piano accompanying a mournful song floated out to greet her before she knocked. Anna paused to listen, frowning as she realised how curiously apt the words were:

> *Yesterday*
> *All my troubles seemed so far away,*
> *Now it looks as though they're here to stay,*
> *Oh, I believe in yesterday ...'*

Registering Anna's knock, Jonathan broke off to call 'Who is it?'

'It's me—Anna!' she shouted through the door.

'Come in,' he invited. 'It isn't locked!'

He turned to smile as she entered the sitting room, his fingers still straying over the keyboard as he crooned the next verse:

'Yesterday,
Love was such an easy game to play,
Now I need a place to hide away . . .'

Anna sat down to wait quietly while he finished the song, but he had caught sight of her face and immediately closed the lid of the piano, got up and came to sit opposite her. 'Is something wrong?' he enquired anxiously, without unnecessary tact.

'No; what makes you . . .?' Anna began, then pulled herself up short as she realised she was already falling into the old routine of self-protection, spurious hardness. Smiling slightly, she returned Jonathan's direct gaze and nodded her head. 'Yes.'

He pursed up his lips. 'You certainly look a bit battered,' he declared roundly.

Anna's smile became wry. 'Thanks a lot.'

'You know what I mean. You always look fine to me, but you're usually so . . . I don't know . . . self-contained. Today you seem positively . . .' he peered more closely into her face, 'less together than usual,' he decided. 'Want to tell me about it?'

Anna shrugged and stared down at her hands. 'I don't know. I'm not used to this kind of thing. Being in this kind of situation,' she muttered.

Jonathan's glance took in the heightened colour in her cheeks, the softened line of her mouth and tender light in her eyes. Something had changed in Anna recently, and he liked it; but he wished fervently that it had anything to do with him, which it obviously had not. 'Let's have it,' he encouraged cheerfully.

'I don't know if you were in last night, Jon,' Anna began cautiously, 'but if you were you might have known I had a visitor.'

'I was out last night, celebrating,' he informed her. 'Hence, if you look carefully, the shadows under the eyes and the faintly greenish tinge to the gills.'

Anna was sidetracked, with some relief. 'Celebrating what? It's not your birthday, is it?' She frowned. 'No, that's in December. So, what . . .?'

'I've sold a song,' he told her happily. 'Could be the big one.'

Anna's smile was instant and sincere, breaking through her dejection like sun dispelling clouds. 'Oh, Jon, I'm so glad! Well done!'

Jonathan sensed that she was only too pleased to have an excuse to lose the thread of what she had been saying, and also that she needed to say it. With surprising strength and intuition, he pushed her back to it. 'Thanks. Now, about your visitor?'

'Oh, that.' Anna shrugged again, her expression slumping. 'Well, you remember I told you about the case involving the boy and his elder brother?'

'The TV mogul, or whatever he was? Of course I do. How's it been going?'

'It's finished. Tied up. Satisfactorily concluded.' Drily, Anna quoted her own official notes. 'Which left me free to invite the said brother over for a meal.'

'Ah!' He was inspecting her shrewdly through his steel-rimmed spectacles.

'You don't look very surprised!' It was almost a challenge, as if she were offended—surely, for goodness' sake, she wasn't quite so transparent?

'Not so hard to guess, Anna. Perhaps I know you better than you think.'

She gazed at him in a new light: perhaps he did. How disconcerting it all was, once you started opening yourself up to people, seeing them for what they really were, allowing them to see you. Had she underestimated the power of Jonathan's personality, even of his feelings, all this time? And if she'd done it with him, then how many others had she done it with? She stared at him ruefully, her brow furrowed. Then she gathered her forces together and made a determined effort to go on. 'Well . . .'

'Presumably you didn't invite him over to discuss the case?' Jonathan prompted. 'Was there something else on your mind? Or was it,' he suggested evenly, 'simply a social call?'

'Both. He wants me to help him make a documentary about Child Psychology, and I've said I would. Also ...' she hesitated, then squared up to him, 'I wanted to see him again, away from the consulting room, so we could find out more about our ...'

'Your budding relationship?' Jonathan tried helpfully, as she faded away again.

'Something like that.' Anna avoided his eye. 'I hoped it was budding,' she explained, flushing as she pushed the honest words out, 'but now I'm not so sure.'

'You mean it didn't feel right, once you were on unprofessional territory?' It was costing Jonathan quite a bit, calmly and affectionately probing the truth out of her, but he pressed on, aware of her need and wanting to help her if he could.

'That's just it.' Anna raised her head to look him full in the face, her eyes glowing, her mouth softly parted. 'It did feel right! It felt fantastic: I wanted it to go on for ever!' Her voice and colour rose on a tide of overwhelming pleasure in the memory. Jonathan's eyebrows arched but he refrained from comment. He had been more accurate than he knew, spotting this change in his mysterious, endearing neighbour. Here was a side of her nature he had certainly never met before.

'So what was the problem?' he enquired, fighting to keep an edge of jealousy out of his tone. Then, catching her expression, he hazarded an intuitive guess. 'You don't mean to tell me this guy doesn't feel the same way about you?' Anna nodded gloomily, collapsing once more into depression. 'Good God! Must be crazy!' For a moment, Jonathan forgot to keep his private reactions to himself for her sake. The times he'd wished he could get this woman to think of him like that, feel about him like that, look at him as she was looking as she recalled this other man!

Anna glanced up at him sharply, almost reading his thoughts and suddenly distracted from her own misery. She had always known Jonathan cared about her, but it had been easy, convenient, to assume his affection to be merely neighbourly. Now that she knew how it felt, how it could hurt, this other feeling, it was no longer safe to assume anything. So, she was in love with Neil; but was Jonathan in love with her? If so, it must be causing him real pain, unburdening all this on to him: it was cruel.

She closed her eyes and rubbed them with a finger and thumb. This was all so complex and difficult! Once you entered the world of the emotions—really entered it, not just on paper or in theory—the ramifications were terrifying. Here was one man, mild and kind and gentle, of whom she was fond enough but who did nothing whatever to stir her up ... but whom, apparently, she in turn stirred up without even realising it. And there was another, very different man, far from mild, not often gentle, who aroused such passions and such empathy within her that he had revitalised her, body and soul. It was ludicrous, ironic. If only the three of them could be sorted out into two distinct, nicely mated pairs, everything fitting and balancing beautifully ...

She regained her equilibrium, determined to help Jonathan now by taking some control again. Either he must let his own feelings out into the open, or he must be able to face them and get over them. The only way to achieve this was by being absolutely frank with him about hers. 'I do love him,' she said quietly, 'and what's more, I like and respect him. If I'd known I was going to say that to you, a few months ago, I'd never have believed it; but a lot's been happening since then. And,' she hardened herself to wade into still deeper water, 'I want him. And I thought he felt the same about me. But as it turned out, he wasn't sure. He needs time to think and feel it through.' That would have to do; no point in going any deeper for the moment. 'Either he'll come round to it, or he won't. I'll get over it, whichever.'

'Hrmph!' Jonathan's grunt was redolent of scepticism, mingled with embarrassment. Then he rallied, folded his arms and gazed solemnly at her. 'I'm sorry, Anna.' His voice was cracked. 'I'm sorry you have to suffer like this. You don't deserve it. For your sake, I hope—I really hope—it comes right for you in the end.'

'Thanks, Jon. And thanks for listening. I feel better already.'

'I'd do a lot more than just listen, Anna, you know that.' Abruptly, he stood up and turned his back on her, shoving his hands into his pockets. 'Since we seem to be exchanging confidences, I suppose you must know how I feel about you.'

It was no more than she had suspected or expected, but Anna bit her lip and held out a hand in his direction. 'Jonathan . . .'

But he had crossed quickly over to the piano, sat on the stool, and was proceeding to express his feelings in the way he knew best, borrowing the words from an old song once popularised by the Beatles:

'Anna,
You call and ask me girl,
To set you free girl,
You say you love him more than me, so I will set you free,
Go with him.
Anna . . .'

His voice tailed off, and for a full minute they brooded in mutual silence. Then he swung round to face her, his expression animated. 'Even if you do get over it, Anna, there's never been a hope in hell you could feel that way about me. Has there?'

She met his gaze with a calm clarity. 'No, Jon. There never has. I never even thought of you like that, and I'm sorry I didn't realise . . .' She swallowed. 'I value your friendship more than I can say; I care about you, I really do. I've been selfish and self-deluding, but I—I don't want this to mean losing you altogether. Perhaps,' her voice softened as she made the suggestion, carefully so as not to hurt him any further, 'perhaps you haven't been seeing me as a real person?'

Jonathan studied her, liking what he saw as much as ever but surprisingly aware of a new resignation to this dimension of affectionate understanding she seemed to be creating between them. Yes, she was right. She had a point. 'I suppose what I've felt for you hasn't been quite real, no,' he confessed hoarsely. 'I'm a romantic soul at heart, and you've always seemed so desirable and yet somehow so—so—I don't know; untouchable, unattainable. Now I know you're human, like the rest of us, I don't like you any less but maybe I see you more clearly . . .'

'Welcome to the human race, is that it?' Anna was smiling. 'Nothing wrong with being a romantic soul,' she heard herself announcing firmly. 'That makes two of us, but we have to face the hard facts of life. Let's help each other keep our feet on the ground from now on, eh, Jon?' Her voice was warm, her hazel eyes direct.

Jonathan turned back to the familiarity of his keyboard, resting his hands on it. Sitting there made him feel not only safe, but also strong, solid and capable. He was going to need to be all three in his future dealings with Anna. No more drooping about like a lovesick teenager. He might have lost a foolish adolescent dream, but he had found a real friend. 'Fair enough, Anna,' he agreed. 'If you can be philosophical, so can I. Just remember, I'm still here if you need a shoulder to cry on.'

'I will. And the same to you. Now,' she became light-hearted, sensing a need to defuse things. 'About this song you've sold. I'm really pleased about it: tell me everything. Which one is it, who's bought it, when do we hear it in the charts?'

This time Jonathan returned her smile; and when he answered her first question it was by singing her the song. It was one of those bitter-sweet ballads he did so well, and its strangely pertinent message and plaintive melody echoed round Anna's head long after she had left him:

> When the thread breaks, your heart aches, your earth
>   quakes;
> When they don't care, and life's bare, I'll be there,
> I'll be there . . .

*   *   *

In their diverse ways, Neil and Daniel were two of a kind. Daniel, with his vigour, enthusiasm and profound insight into human nature; Neil, swinging now into his stride to display a charismatic power, a dynamic vision which had everyone concerned (including several eminent academic experts) running around at his command. Halfway through that first week Anna formally introduced them, and within days they had the material and the participants well in hand. Quietly joining in, but keeping a low profile, Anna marvelled as their combined energy and drive pushed aside obstacles, sucked in anyone who might be useful and spat out those who wouldn't. In a surprisingly short time an end product began to emerge in a recognisable form.

Days melted into weeks. Anna went on counselling clients, writing reports, baking cakes, paying occasional visits to friends and relatives—some of whom, the more perceptive ones, were puzzled at the change in her. Meanwhile, several times a week, she was involved with the making of the documentary at some level or other. Every time she saw Neil, or knew she would be seeing him, she was consumed with a conflict of dread and longing; but outwardly she kept both under strict control, simply giving all she could to the project and behaving with as much dignity and serenity as she could muster when she confronted him.

For his part, Neil's public attitude to Anna was understated and dispassionate, and it seemed to her that he made sure there were no chances for a private attitude to appear at all. Almost all the time, they were surrounded by colleagues, in her profession as well as his, and he treated her much as he treated them: with an easy, masterful courtesy. He was not above using his considerable charm to get just what he required from team members, television crew and contributors alike. These flashes of deliberate male impact, especially when it came to the women participants, were never lost on Anna as she watched from the other side of a studio or organised an interview or a staged session in someone's consulting room. She felt trapped and impotent, forced to witness those sensitive lips curving into their vivid smile, the crinkling corners of the lucid blue eyes as they focused sharply on a face, those absorbed moments when firm fingers pushed through blond hair in a gesture she knew and responded to at a helplessly uncontrollable level.

But although her heart lurched and her stomach somersaulted whenever contact between them became inevitable and Neil addressed her, perhaps across a table or even a room, she kept her outer self as poised and objective as his. She could only deal with the cool blue eyes, the friendly but breezy deep voice, by replying with a mechanical stiffness which ignored the crying out of her feelings.

Once, when they were several weeks into the film, as Anna gazed out of the tall window of a spacious room they were using at a famous clinic in leafy Hampstead, she started at the sudden weight of a hand on her shoulder. She knew at once, from her body's response, whose hand it was. Swinging round, she confronted Neil: his expression nonchalant but his eyes strangely veiled as if to prevent any emotion escaping in the midst of such industrious activity.

'Anna?' The hand on her shoulder, her name on his lips, recalled the times when that mouth and those fingers had invaded and explored her body, creating a shape from the formless mass she had been, moulding her yielding flesh and spirit into maturity, plumbing the depths of her adult desires at last.

Steeling herself against such treacherous recollections, she faced him serenely. 'Yes, Neil? Something I can do?' Her eyes searched the room, where various contributors were fussing about. 'Hasn't Professor Imberg turned up yet from Cambridge? She was supposed to be here half an hour ago.'

'No panic.' He smiled, slightly but directly, causing a frisson to run through her. 'It's all running like clockwork. I've got a few spare minutes, and I wanted to come and thank you for all your help. If it wasn't for your part in it, I'm absolutely sure it wouldn't be going half as well. We work together like a veteran team, wouldn't you say?' He took a step back and thrust his hands into the pockets of the smart, light, loose-cut trousers he wore on these stuffy working days. He was so cool, physically so much in charge, no matter how sultry or oppressive the conditions.

Anna stared at him, disconcerted, trying to read his obscure signals. Was he trying to tell her something, or should she simply take his compliment at its face value? Finally, regretfully, she opted for the latter, and smiled sweetly up at him. 'It was all part of our original bargain, Neil. No need for thanks: I'm only . . .'

His eyes darkened to a bruised blue-black, filling her with anxiety. '. . . only fulfilling your official function? Doing your job? We know all about that, don't we?' He turned away. As she had done before on a similar occasion, Anna clutched at his arm in remorseful panic. Why couldn't she learn—even now?

'Neil . . .'

He halted, his expression set hard. 'Yes?'

People were milling about, and she looked around her, moistening her dry lips with the tip of her tongue; then she lost her nerve. This was neither the time nor the place. 'I only wondered—how's Chris? I've seen the social workers' reports, of course, and they're fine; I know he was just put on a year's probation. But how is he really, at home—in himself?' She was genuinely eager to know.

Neil gazed at her for a moment, assessing, studying. Then he smiled, clearly also opting for the easier way out. 'He's great: better than ever. As I'm sure you know full well, you performed a minor miracle there, Anna,' he observed on a dry note. 'And not only with Chris. Neither of us will ever be quite the same again.'

'Ne-il!' One of his research assistants was calling him, waving a frantic arm from across the room. 'Can you come here? There's a mix-up with the script order!'

'Coming!' He waved cheerfully back, then muttered for Anna's ear alone, 'They couldn't organise a drinking party in a brewery if I didn't stand over them!' She grinned, elated to feel that she was singled out, taken into his confidence at least, even if it was only in this working context. Then he added tersely: 'About Chris and me: you should be pleased with your efforts, flower. They were magnificent.'

Swinging round before she could find an answer, he plunged back into the throng, dominant among the rest, leaving her to stare after him, eyes wide and lips parted. Funny, she mused suddenly, how it used to irritate her, back in the bad old days, when he called her 'flower'. Patronising, sexist, unnecessary, she used to complain to herself, while having too much restraint to say so outright. Now simply hearing him say it—so characteristic, so ironic—set her nerve-endings jangling along with everything else that was so particularly him. She sighed, smiling ruefully to herself even as she lamented the final passing of her old, impervious self; then she stood up straight and marched back into the fray to get on with the job in hand.

Through the stuffy summer, everyone at the clinic gave of their best for Neil while keeping up their caseloads at the same time. As the days dwindled into a golden autumn, their part in the film was finally complete and life returned to normal when it went off to be spliced and edited. Anna's profound regret at the end of the regular contact with Neil was tinged with a slight relief, just as the trees were touched with a hint of brown. The strain was beginning to tell. She had not taken a holiday for well over a year, and it had been a trying twelve months. At weekends she immersed herself in fits of cooking; sometimes she watched television with Jonathan and his newly acquired, extremely sweet girlfriend, enjoying their quiet company and Jonathan's obvious happiness. Her body cried out for rest but her mind struggled against sleep. She grew paler and thinner, her eyes shadowed, her already prominent bone structure more pronounced than ever.

This did not go unheeded by her colleagues. Pam was

the first to put it into words. 'Anna, love,' she announced as Anna reported for duty one Friday morning, tired but punctual. 'You're looking really washed out.'

Anna's mouth tightened grimly. 'Thanks, Pam.'

'Don't be silly, I'm not criticising: I'm just worried about you, that's all. So's Daniel. We were talking about you yesterday, and he was saying . . .'

'Oh, you were, were you?' In her exhaustion Anna became touchier than usual. 'Nice to know I'm so fascinating,' she growled, poring over the desk diary.

'Come off it, love. It's not like you to be so paranoid. He was only saying you've worked ever so hard on Mr Tyrell's film, and now it's over you should take a break. It's ages since you did, and you certainly deserve one.'

'Oh yes? And who's going to see all these customers if I disappear?'

'We always manage, you know that. Daniel's holiday isn't booked till the spring, and Gill and I have already had ours. I thought I ought to warn you, anyway,' Pam added, bustling about her own business. 'Daniel's planning to talk you into taking a holiday, and he can be very persuasive when he wants to.'

Anna forced a wan smile. They had her best interests at heart and it was ungracious not to acknowledge it. 'Thanks, Pam. I'll be ready for the attack!' The first clients were arriving, so she slung her bag over her shoulder, picked up her briefcase and set off through the door to the consulting rooms.

I'll say Daniel can be very persuasive, her mind droned as she sorted out her files for the day. It was his damned persuasion that had got her into all this hassle in the first place. Perhaps they were right though: she needed a break. But where would she go? She was due for at least a month off, but she hardly ever took her full allocation of leave. She had never been much of a one for solitary travelling. She could stay at home, of course, or visit her parents . . .

The first client was announced, and she braced herself for another day. Time enough to climb that hurdle when Daniel actually threw it in front of her. But long before he had the chance, a much higher one reared up in her path: that afternoon she received a 'phone call from Neil.

Over the weeks, she had almost succeeded in convincing herself she was unlikely to hear from him again. She had served her purpose, and doubtless he had decided he had done the right thing in rejecting her, and was duly relieved to be off the hook. In any case, the ball was in his court: the next move was his, and she could only wait and suffer, suspended, her fierce responses to him in the flesh dulling slowly, painfully, into a tight hard knot of internal anguish.

Her real reaction to his voice was an almost total physical and nervous convulsion; but she was so schooled in the art of hiding it by now that she kept her own voice quite bland. 'This is a surprise! What can I do for you?'

'I wonder.' He was no less calm or enigmatic, and she wondered helplessly whether it was a game they were both playing, or whether he had no need to pretend.

'How does the film look?' She was searching desperately for mild conversation.

'That's what I'm here to say. It's finished and it looks great. Bloody good, Anna.' His tone was vibrant with satisfaction, and she had to respond with pleased sympathy rather than resentment. He had deserved his success, worked hard for it.

'Well done, Neil! I'm delighted to hear it.'

'An award-winning documentary, if ever I made one!' he declared, as confident as ever. 'And I couldn't have done it without you and your colleagues. You know that. I want to thank you all, especially you, Anna. You were really wonderful.'

'I really enjoyed it, Neil,' she assured him truthfully. 'It was a most enlightening experience. I wouldn't have missed it for anything.'

'None of it?' There was a suggestion of wickedness in his tone now, and she clenched up again. That was below the belt, especially as she couldn't see his face.

'How do you mean?' she countered starchily.

'I mean,' he explained, 'it needn't be over yet. I've got the first video of the great work, and I'd like you to be the first to see it. And I assume you have not succumbed to the pleasures of the medium and fixed yourself up with a set?'

'No,' she stated firmly. 'And I don't even know anyone with a video recorder.'

'Oh, yes, you do,' he corrected heavily. 'You know me, and I've got two VTRs.'

'Yes, well, I suppose you would have.' She waited, breathless, for his next move.

'So you can come over here and watch it with us, can't you?' He was so smooth and brisk, anyone would think she made a habit of visiting his home. 'Chris is dying to see you again. He keeps getting at me for not asking you over. He really misses you, Anna. You became a very special person in his life.'

And what about you? her mind was screaming, so loudly she was sure he must hear it; but all she said was, 'I miss him, too. I got very fond of him, though I'm not supposed to say that about a client.' It was no more than the truth, after all.

'So, are you coming or aren't you?' He was abrasive, pushing for a decision.

Anna knew full well they were talking about more than simply viewing their film. He had something to say to her, and she could only guess hopelessly at what it was. Steeling herself, she took the plunge. 'Of course I'll come. I can't wait to see the programme, and I'm sure they won't show it for months yet.'

'Quite right. It's scheduled for early next year. Come over for lunch on Sunday and we can watch it after that.' He was still giving nothing whatever away.

'Lunch? Are you sure? What about Mrs R—won't she mind?'

'Stop wriggling, Anna. Mrs R will be overwhelmed to entertain you. Time has not tarnished your shining reputation in this household. She keeps dropping broad hints that it's high time we invited you over. She and

Chris are a positive conspiracy.'

He made it sound as if he was only asking her in order to please them. 'Then I'd better come.' The words were clipped. 'Now, I've got a client due, Neil. I'll have to go; will twelve-thirty do?'

'Twelve-thirty will be ideal. See you, flower.' He rang off. It was done.

November had crept up on them, and Sunday dawned cold and damp. Anna put on brown cords and a warm orange sweatshirt, and stepped out of her car outside the handsome Canonbury residence, looking a lot calmer than she felt. It was amazing how you could go through the motions, fulfil such normal functions, when you knew your future was likely to be in the balance. Neil welcomed her, even more casual in faded denims and an old hand-knit jumper. Behind him, similarly attired, hovered a beaming Christopher, his face a study in open delight.

'Hallo, Chris.' Anna smiled warmly at him, noting how well he looked, how relaxed and filled out, shaping up more than ever like his brother.

'Great to see you, Anna.' There would be no more lurking in his room for Chris, she knew. He was right here in the thick of things, and intended to stay there.

'Anna.' Laconically polite, Neil stood aside as she entered, then closed the door behind her, his face and voice inscrutable. 'Glad you could make it.'

'Neil.' Her quick smile did not register the burning and tingling she felt on seeing him again, on brushing past him in the hall. 'I couldn't refuse an invitation to inspect our work of art, now could I?'

'I should think not. Chris has seen it, haven't you, Chris?'

'It's really good,' the boy told her eagerly. 'You'll like it, Anna.'

'I'm sure I will.' In spite of her guard, she was merging into their atmosphere of mutual affection and support. It was new and tangible, and enclosed her, drew her in; and she had no will to prevent it.

Mrs R, busy in her kitchen, greeted Anna like a long-lost relative. 'It's lovely to see you again, Doctor. I've been dying to thank you for what you did for Chris. For them both ... I can't tell you ...' Her voice dropped to a conspiratorial whisper; Neil had disappeared to organise seating in the dining room. 'This has been a different house. Chris is a different boy. I don't know how you did it!'

'I'm glad it worked, anyway; that's the main thing.' Anna smiled. 'And please,' she added as Neil returned and the older woman began to dish up the vegetables, 'call me Anna. I'm here strictly off-duty; let's forget about all the rest.'

Over succulent roast lamb and all the trimmings, the four of them chatted easily about a range of subjects. Chris was lively and alert, Mrs R bustling with good humour and pleasure in entertaining Anna at her table, just as Neil had said she would be. Neil himself was amiable, attentive and personal, his smile charming, his conversation witty: the other side of the coin from the tough public figure in rigorous action. Any deeper than that, Anna simply could not read in him. She was beginning to suspect he had invited her over there to show her how he wanted her to fit into his life in future: as a welcome family friend, a visitor, but no more.

It was a convenient way out, a useful scenario, but it would never do for her. His presence only triggered off those same old messages, sharpened rather than dulled with passing time. Dominant but content in his own home setting, the parts of the man fell into place, a symmetrical whole, and she loved all of them. Seeing him that way once in a while as an outsider, Anna knew she would never be able to stand it. All or nothing, it would have to be; and the realisation was a painful one.

As they reached the fresh fruit salad, Chris was regaling her with his current activities and future plans. 'I've started at the Tech, doing eight O-levels,' he pronounced proudly. Then he looked her straight in the eye. 'After that I want to study psychology at university.'

Three pairs of eyes watched for Anna's reaction. For a moment she was nonplussed, but then she broke into a grin. 'What a fantastic idea, Chris! I like it!'

Neil was clearly pleased with his brother's decision. 'I told him he should make a great shrink,' he said solemnly, 'especially after all that useful work experience.'

To Anna's slight consternation, Mrs R and Chris vanished after lunch to do the washing up, refusing her offers of help. She was left to follow Neil upstairs as he showed her round the rest of the house. Its tasteful period simplicity continued through every room, comfortable and dignified—apart from Christopher's modern teenage lair. It was a beautiful house, spacious but manageable, cosy but stately, far from the bare bleak place the social workers had described all that time ago. Either they had been wrong, Anna reflected, or the new atmosphere between its inmates had permeated the walls and the furnishings, bringing them life and warmth.

Finally Neil led her up the topmost flight of stairs into an attic studio which stretched the full width and length of the house. Decorated and equipped in much more contemporary style, it was flooded with light from dormer windows set into the slope of the roof. Enclosing and inviting, with couches and cushions, it was also soundproofed and set up as an office with desk, files, shelves full of books. An impressive assortment of audio and video machinery in one corner announced it to be Neil's recording and viewing area: his private workspace.

'My den.' He waved an expansive hand around it. 'Like it?'

Anna had wandered over to the only window she could reach, standing on tiptoe to peer out, escaping from the powerful pull of his proximity as best she could. 'It's marvellous, Neil. What an incredible view! And it's so peaceful.' Her glance ranged the room, so

indelibly stamped with Neil's mark. Her ears drank in
the silence, so far above the throb of London, cut off
from the rest of the house. It was an eyrie, a closed cell,
and they were alone in it together. A sixth sense told
her that no one ever disturbed Neil while he was up
here, whether he was alone or not.

He was silent, leaning on the wall at the opposite end
of the room, but she became acutely aware that his eyes
were upon her, and turned slowly, almost reluctantly, to
meet them. They lingered lazily on her countenance and
then down over her body. Suddenly free from anxiety
and inhibition, she allowed hers to do the same,
drinking him in as if to quench an intolerable thirst.
What did it matter what he was going to say? They
were here now, and this moment was enough in itself.

For endless seconds the two of them were frozen,
polarised into their perpetual corners: Neil and Anna,
eternally separated by acres of wall-to-wall empty
space. Then they were both moving, simultaneously
propelled together by a force which came from within
them and outside them and all around; meeting in the
middle of that space in a soundless gasp which none the
less seemed to Anna to rock the room, the house, the
city, the whole world.

Their merging was elemental, so long delayed that it
was violent. There was no place for words. Thought
flew out of the window, to be replaced by instinct again.
Neil's body, the sight, the sound and feel of it, became
Anna's only reality, her frame of existence. Her heart
sang until she felt it would burst, as she gave way at last
to pent-up emotions, expressing them gladly and
generously in the only language that really makes sense.

Gentle at first, Neil grew urgent and then demanding;
but her own demands were a match for his. When he
took her, there was no shock or pain, only a whirling
rising tide of sensation, an explosion and a long cry
from far away: a timeless duet of fulfilment.

Afterwards, as the sky began to darken outside the
slanting windows, they clung to each other, relishing
that unique closeness and tranquillity. Sinking deep into

floor cushions, Anna snuggled against Neil, revelling in the hard pulsating strength of him, the sheer male vitality of him; marvelling in the knowledge, instilled into her now for all time, of his possession. That unbearable, wonderful power of it, reducing all other power to the merest bagatelle, a pale reflection and no more. Never mind what happened next: there would be no regrets.

He raised himself on one elbow to gaze down at her. 'Anna? Are you awake?'

She focused sleepy eyes on to the familiar features, as vital to her as facets of herself. 'Of course I am. Did you think you'd bored me to sleep?'

'Hardly.' He bent to kiss her softly on the cheek, the eyes, the nose, with a new teasing tenderness. 'But you do look tired. Haven't you been well? You've lost weight, haven't you?' His eyes were deep with concern as they probed hers.

'Are you complaining?' She smiled up at him.

'No way. There's plenty left to enjoy.' His arms tightened about her. 'I thought I might have overworked you. Or perhaps,' he suggested archly, 'you've been missing me? Fading away without me? Is that it?'

Her own gaze became deeply serious as she prepared herself to be candid. 'If you must know, Neil, I've been in hell. Frantic, lonely, pining. Ever since . . .'

'My dearest girl! My flower, my precious Anna! What have I put you through, with my ridiculous scruples? I thought I was protecting you, when I realised how—how vulnerable you were. But when I went away and thought it through, I came to the conclusion I'd been protecting myself. What you were offering, in your honest, beautiful way, was too much like a commitment. I knew that, and I wasn't ready to take it on. Oh, I meant the things I said . . .' his expression darkened as he forced the self-deprecating words out, 'but basically all that was just an easier way of telling you I needed time. Easier on me,' he added harshly. 'Harder on you.'

Anna could scarcely believe what she was hearing, but she kept the burgeoning joy at bay a little longer.

'All the time we were making the film,' she whispered, 'you were so stony, so self-contained. I just couldn't tell what was going on in your mind.'

'We had to get the damned thing done.' His tone hardened. 'Anyway, you didn't do so badly at keeping cool, yourself.'

'It wasn't easy,' Anna admitted, exhaustion hitting her all over again at the memory.

'My poor, poor lady.' He bent to kiss her again. 'And stronger, and with more integrity, than a dozen men. I was a fool, to take risks with something so—so delicate and uncertain. How can I ever make it up to you?' he groaned, burying his face in her neck.

'You're doing that now, Neil,' she assured him quietly, suddenly calm and strong again in her delight. 'And what's more, I don't want to hear any more of this sackcloth and ashes stuff. I respected your motives, that night; I understood exactly what you meant. We both needed to feel our way further into things, before we took that final step. You were right. We both had to be absolutely sure. I thought I was, then, and I hoped you were, but now . . .'

'Anna,' he interrupted, levering himself free so that he could look into her face. 'Are you sure, now? What I've put you through, it hasn't changed your mind?'

She shook her head, wrinkling her nose at him. 'How can you doubt it, after what's just happened? It wouldn't say much for my—what was it?—integrity if I wasn't, would it?' Her gaze was clear, steady on his. 'And you, Neil? Are *you* sure?'

'I've never been so certain of anything in my life,' he stated emphatically. 'Of course, I started loving you way back—God knows when—all that sparring and skirmishing we did when Chris was first sent to you. I was so alarmed at my own reactions to you, Dr Coleman, that I withdrew my own brother from your tender ministrations.' He grinned crookedly. 'But Chris wasn't letting me get away with that. Fate must have been guiding him, pulling him further and further down into depression and despair.'

Anna laughed outright. 'How fanciful, Mr Tyrell!' Reaching out, she pulled him to her, hugging him. 'Well, perhaps it was all for the best, in the end.'

'I should say it was.' His reply was no less vehement for being muffled against her. 'Thanks to you, I'm a new man, at every level, as you very well know. You've hooked me, body and soul. You've achieved what I thought no woman ever would. I'm in love with you, and I intend to go on being in love with you for a very long time.'

'Oh, Neil!' The happiness was so intense it hurt. Anna could hardly bear it. Clinging to him, she kissed him passionately, pushing him down among the cushions, wanton, abandoned, ecstatic—finally freed, once and for all, to be herself.

'Steady on, woman!' He kicked and squirmed ineffectually. 'I've heard of female domination but this is ridiculous! Help! Rape!' But no one heard him in his soundproofed den, and he was forced to endure her attentions until more primitive instincts took over and he seized control; and it was even more of a revelation to them both than the last time.

A long, calm while later, it was Anna's turn to nudge Neil into alertness. 'I think we should be watching this film,' she mumbled drowsily, 'or they'll be up here . . .'

'Don't worry, flower.' His hand was gently stroking the curve of her breast. 'They know better than to interrupt me when I'm busy up here. Plenty of time for all that. We can spend the rest of our life watching programmes together—making them, too, if you like the idea.'

She giggled, wondering whether Mrs R and Chris had the slightest suspicion as to what Neil might be busy at just now. She decided they probably did, and then became serious again. 'I think I'll leave making the films to you. But I'd certainly like to be around to watch you make them, and see them afterwards, if that's what you want.'

He regarded her gravely, peacefully. 'That's what I want, Anna. I want you to come and live with me, and carry on with your wonderful works while I carry on with mine. I want to look after you, see that you never get all pale and thin and forlorn again. I want you to look after me, and both of us to look after Chris. And Mrs R to look after us all. Okay?' He made it all sound so simple, such a logical idyll.

'But what will they say? Won't they mind? If I move in here, I mean?'

'They'll both be delighted. They both think you're the greatest thing since sliced bread. Not that Mrs R approves of sliced bread,' he added, grinning.

'But I like to do lots of cooking, when I have time. Won't she feel put out?'

'Not if I know Mrs R, and I do. She can cook for us all during the week, and at weekends the kitchen can be all yours, whenever you want. She's always said she could do with more weekends off to see her family. You could be helping her out.'

'Well ...' It sounded like heaven, but Anna was naturally cautious. 'We could give it a try, I suppose. I'd love to come and live with you all, I do know that.'

'And perhaps one day,' Neil was nuzzling her bare neck, 'if you can bring yourself to sacrifice your independent status, you might even consider marrying me.'

'Being married doesn't mean sacrificing your independence!' Anna protested heatedly. 'I'm always telling my clients' parents that, when they come with marital problems.'

'Then we'll be married as soon as you like. We'll take a very long, very comprehensive honeymoon, somewhere steamy and sinful, in the middle of winter.'

'Yes, I'd like that.' Anna smiled her agreement. There was a private element to her smile: she'd obviously be taking that well-earned long holiday after all.

'One condition, Doctor.' She glanced up, questioning, at the solemn note in his voice. 'We invite your parents to the wedding, and both get to know them properly.'

Anna thought about this, and nodded thoughtfully. 'Fair enough; yes, you're right.'

'You'll get used to that,' he assured her airily. 'Now, we'd better go down and join them for tea, or they'll think we've entered a suicide pact. And, delectable as you look like that, I suggest you put on at least a few clothes, or I might get other ideas and we'll still be here by breakfast time.'

Anna stuck out her tongue at him and began searching around for her scattered garments. Neil sat cross-legged on the cushion, surveying her lovingly, a faint smile playing at the corners of his mouth. 'To think,' he observed, 'I'm doomed to spend the rest of my days being thoroughly Anna-lysed.'

Anna groaned as she zipped up her jeans, glaring at him in mock disgust. 'You've been saving that one up for weeks!' she accused. 'Anway, I've heard it before, from other witty customers.'

'Actually, it was Chris who first came out with it,' Neil admitted, still watching her as if he could not bear to tear his eyes away.

'And will you mind?' Anna crouched beside him, her arms creeping around him of their own accord. 'Having your own personal analyst on the premises?'

'Mind?' He pretended to consider it, while she nibbled his ear. 'Why the hell should I mind? Especially since she happens to be the most beautiful, the most accomplished, and by far the sexiest example of her species in the world.'

ROMANCE

Variety is the spice of romance

Each month, Mills & Boon publish new romances. New stories about people falling in love. A world of variety in romance — from the best writers in the romantic world. Choose from these titles in March.

RECKLESS Amanda Carpenter
MAN IN THE PARK Emma Darcy
AN UNBREAKABLE BOND Robyn Donald
ONE IN A MILLION Sandra Field
DIPLOMATIC AFFAIR Claire Harrison
POWER POINT Rowan Kirby
DARK BETRAYAL Patricia Lake
NO LONGER A DREAM Carole Mortimer
A SCARLET WOMAN Margaret Pargeter
A LASTING KIND OF LOVE Catherine Spencer
*BLUEBELLS ON THE HILL Barbara McMahon
*RETURN TO FARAWAY Valerie Parv

On sale where you buy paperbacks. If you require further information or have any difficulty obtaining them, write to: Mills & Boon Reader Service, PO Box 236, Thornton Road, Croydon, Surrey CR9 3RU, England.

*These two titles are available *only* from Mills & Boon Reader Service.

Mills & Boon
the rose of romance

Take 4
Exciting Books
Absolutely
FREE

Love, romance, intrigue... all are captured for you by Mills & Boon's top-selling authors. By becoming a regular reader of Mills & Boon's Romances you can enjoy 6 superb new titles every month plus a whole range of special benefits: your very own personal membership card, a free monthly newsletter packed with recipes, competitions, exclusive book offers and a monthly guide to the stars, plus extra bargain offers and big cash savings.

AND an Introductory FREE GIFT for YOU.
Turn over the page for details.

As a special introduction we will send you four exciting Mills & Boon Romances Free and without obligation when you complete and return this coupon.

At the same time we will reserve a subscription to Mills & Boon Reader Service for you. Every month, you will receive 6 of the very latest novels by leading Romantic Fiction authors, delivered direct to your door. You don't pay extra for delivery — postage and packing is always completely Free. There is no obligation or commitment — you can cancel your subscription at any time.

You have nothing to lose and a whole world of romance to gain.

Just fill in and post the coupon today to **MILLS & BOON READER SERVICE, FREEPOST, P.O. BOX 236, CROYDON, SURREY CR9 9EL.**

Please Note:- READERS IN SOUTH AFRICA write to Mills & Boon, Postbag X3010, Randburg 2125, S. Africa.

- -

FREE BOOKS CERTIFICATE

To: Mills & Boon Reader Service, FREEPOST, P.O. Box 236, Croydon, Surrey CR9 9EL.

Please send me, free and without obligation, four Mills & Boon Romances, and reserve a Reader Service Subscription for me. If I decide to subscribe I shall, from the beginning of the month following my free parcel of books, receive six new books each month for £6.60, post and packing free. If I decide not to subscribe, I shall write to you within 10 days. The free books are mine to keep in any case. I understand that I may cancel my subscription at any time simply by writing to you. I am over 18 years of age.

Please write in BLOCK CAPITALS.

Signature _____

Name _____

Address _____

_____ Post code _____

SEND NO MONEY — TAKE NO RISKS.

Please don't forget to include your Postcode.

Remember, postcodes speed delivery. Offer applies in UK only and is not valid to present subscribers. Mills & Boon reserve the right to exercise discretion in granting membership. If price changes are necessary you will be notified.

6R   Offer expires 31st March 1986.

EP86